THE
Three Princes
OF
Serendip

THE
THREE PRINCES
OF
SERENDIP

Elizabeth Jamison Hodges

drawings by Joan Berg

ATHENEUM *1966* NEW YORK

Library of Congress catalog card number 64-11887
Published simultaneously in Canada
by McClelland & Stewart Ltd.
Manufactured in the United States of America
Printed by The Murray Printing Company,
Forge Village, Massachusetts
Bound by H. Wolff, New York
Designed by David Rogers
First Printing January 1964
Second Printing March 1966

Honoring my father and my mother,

William Lemmon Hodges

and

Elizabeth Jamison Hodges

Contents

THE *Three Princes* OF *Serendip*

THE

Stern Decree

Long, long ago in a land far off at the end of the earth, there lived a great ruler, whose name was Jaiya. His was the island kingdom of Serendip, where tall trees grew on emerald mountains, rich farms flourished, and lotus blossoms delighted the eyes of men.

Early in his reign, three sons were born to Jaiya; and on the day each entered the world, a strange bird, with golden wings and eyes like fire, dipped low out of the sky. It was seen, however, by only a handful of children in a mountain valley near the ancient and holy Peak of Great Serenity. They were looking up and exclaimed with joy at the marvelous sight.

The other people did not raise their eyes because they were laughing and feasting on sweet keribath and plump reddish plantains. Jaiya missed it, too, for although he rejoiced in his sons, he had many burdens which made his head bend low with anxiety.

In his day, the land was bountiful; but it had not always been so. The rains which fell upon his realm came chiefly in a single season; and once, vast stretches of the country for many months each year had been dry and uncomely.

And so they might have remained had not Jaiya built immense tanks as large as lakes. When great downpours drenched the earth, these reservoirs filled so high that there was fresh water for all the people, their farms and flowers.

The king was constantly concerned to see that his royal officials attended to the repair of the great tanks and also kept the thousands of canals that wound between them unclogged. The ruler of Serendip knew that were it not for his vigilance, some who were charged with the care of these waters might easily grow fat and neglectful. Then distress and suffering would walk into his kingdom.

Since the demands of his throne were so great, and because Jaiya knew that he could not rule forever, he pondered deeply the matter of education for his three sons. Virtue, wisdom, and science, these he wished them to learn in order some day to be worthy rulers themselves. Therefore, being a wise man, he asked even wiser men than he, of his own country and of other lands, to come and teach them.

Very few from abroad dared approach his island realm, however, because great dragons, monsters of the sea, inhabited the wide ocean lanes around the land of Serendip. Many times Jaiya had invited famous storytellers and philosophers to his kingdom; but more often than not, they, out of terror, had refused to come. And even now when he urged renowned teachers of the world to visit him, that they might help to instruct his royal sons, only a very few dared to cross the infested seas.

These, it was clear, were not only wise but full of courage. So the King of Serendip welcomed each with high honors and many civilities.

During the years of study no one disturbed the young princes or their teachers. Day after day the lessons continued until at last the royal brothers had grown to full height and seemed ready to be called men. Then Jaiya summoned their instructors to ask how much his sons had learned.

Wearing a garment of white silk, the king received the teachers with royal courtesy in the hall of state of his palace at Anuradhapura. Here, while musicians of the court played upon their flutes and drums, he bade the philosophers speak.

"O, Noble King," the oldest teacher said, raising his voice to be heard more clearly above the music, "the royal princes have been well instructed in religion, grammar, and the management of elephants. Your Majesty's first son, Prince Balakrama, excels in logic and has an absorbing interest in all living things. Your second royal son, Prince Vijayo, is skilled in science and is a lover of the arts. As for Prince Rajahsingha, Your Majesty's third son, he is full of courage yet a man of peace and knowing in government. Besides this, they are all proficient in languages, poetry, and music."

"Now that last is a good thing," said Jaiya, frowning because a flutist had just played a wrong note. Then, with a little smile in his eyes, he nodded for the teacher to continue.

"No one, however," the philosopher said with a low bow, "can be more aware than Your Noble Self of the many difficulties to be overcome in the ruling of Serendip. So it is our judgment that the royal princes should perfect their education by traveling abroad."

This counsel seemed good to Jaiya, but he wished to test his sons himself in order to hear with his own ears how wise they were and how ready to learn abroad. So he called them one by one and addressed each separately.

Balakrama came first, riding upon Kandula, his favorite elephant. Caparisoned with splendid trappings of red and gold, the creature bore the prince to the royal palace. There the young man dismounted swiftly, and, pausing only long enough to stroke Kandula gently on his great trunk, hurried within and bowed before the king.

"My son," Jaiya said, "as you can well see, I am growing older with every day. My time of strength may not be long, and this land must not be left without a ruler. Therefore, looking toward the future, I now offer you the government of this kingdom. Keep the teachings of Buddha ever in your heart and strive for the tranquillity and contentment of all our people."

Saying these words, Jaiya raised the crown from his head as if he were about to place it on that of his oldest son. Balakrama was amazed. However, he was a prince with sharp eyes, and he could also see with his heart. He noticed that when the king lifted the crown, he still held it tightly in his own fingers.

So he answered, "I am honored, Sir, that Your Majesty should have so great a trust in me, and I am grateful for your noble counsel. If an ant, however, should come up out of his nest, would he be fit to govern this vast realm? Compared to Your Majesty, I am only a tiny ant without strength and practice. Always I have tried to follow your royal wishes, but in this instance, I beg to be excused."

The king rejoiced in the modesty and sense of these words, but he was careful not to show his pleasure. Instead he kept a solemn expression as he let Balakrama go and sent for Vijayo.

This prince, with a little sigh, put down the scroll he was reading at the moment and hastily presented himself with a low bow before the king. To his second son Jaiya made the same offer, and, in doing so, stood up as if to allow the youth to sit in his place upon the throne.

Vijayo, a prince with keen ears, who could also hear with his heart, noticed that the king's voice was far from feeble. Besides, he felt sure that his father would be happy to rule until the end of his days.

He said therefore, "Your Majesty is both generous

and wise. I, however, am like a drop of water which may disappear in the heat of the day or be merged with its fellows in the vast seas of your dominions. Besides, I am only Your Majesty's second son and have an older brother. So with deep respect, I beg to decline your royal offer."

The king was delighted by the reply of Prince Vijayo; but he took pains not to show his approval, and called for his third son. When the summons reached Rajahsingha, he was visiting a court of justice. But he hurried to the king and bowed low. Jaiya addressed him in the same way he had spoken to his brothers.

Now the youngest prince had a brave heart as well as a brave mind. He listened and was astonished. Then, although he felt that the king might be displeased if his offer were not accepted, Rajahsingha spoke his own thoughts freely.

"O Noble King," he said, "is it wise for one so young to accept a dignity so large? I know of no heat greater than the sun. Also I believe that no one can govern our country so well as Your Majesty. Besides, I am only a third son and have two older brothers. Pray, allow me to refuse."

Jaiya was pleased beyond measure because each of his three sons had proved himself to be a prince of both modesty and wisdom. Nevertheless, the king did not permit the expression of his face to show the deep sentiments of his heart. Nor did he deem it fitting to bestow upon his sons honor, riches, or power.

Instead, like their wise teachers, he decided the

princes were now ready to perfect their education by travel in the great world and at the same time to undertake the solution of one of the most serious problems that plagued his kingdom. So the very next day he called them to him again. Believing that they might be too happy in Serendip to wish to leave, and knowing, because of the love he bore them, that his own will in the matter might otherwise weaken, he spoke with sternness.

"Wisdom," he said, "is deeper than the sea. So you have much to learn before you are ready to become great rulers. Therefore, I command you to leave Anuradhapura in no more than seven days and to quit the land of Serendip within fifteen. You are to travel through the heights, the valleys, and the great beyonds of the world in order to gain the character, the wisdom, and the right to rule. And more than this, you are to do."

In some dismay, but keeping silent, the three princes stood before their father.

"Ancients have said," Jaiya continued, "that once the mists of yesterday were marvelously distilled into a magic formula. This was written in one hundred lines of verse upon a single scroll. Named *Death to Dragons,* these lines contained the secret of a potent liquid which, if poured into an ocean lane, could utterly destroy upon the instant, all dangerous monsters there."

The princes had not heard of this before and were filled with wonder and excitement.

"Had we that formula," Jaiya said, "though its

words may be obscure and difficult, I believe that we could possess the mixture it describes. Therefore, my sons, I command that in your travels you search out this magic poem that we may rid our shores of all the dragons that have plagued us for so long.

"Moreover," continued Jaiya, "you are expressly charged not to return without my permission. Only if you acquit yourselves in a worthy manner, will you be allowed to walk once more in the land of Serendip. Therefore, send me word of your adventures and let me know where my messengers may find you; but until you clearly merit royal power, it is not fit that you should look upon my face again."

The princes were young and liked the thought of travel, but they also had a deep affection for the king and felt uneasy about leaving him in so sudden a manner and under so stern a decree. Hopefully, they asked for a longer time in which to make ready for their journey; but Jaiya refused to change his order and quickly turned about to hide his tears as his three sons took their leave.

After this with heavy hearts and anxious thoughts, the brothers made ready to depart. They took assumed names and put on garments of plain white cotton so that they would not appear as princes. Balakrama bade farewell to his mighty Kandula, and the three brothers rode upon other elephants with no elaborate trappings. So simply did they travel that they could easily have been taken for young mahouts, charged with the care of the elephants, rather than for the sons of a king.

As they departed through the city they passed a

nine-storied monastery with brazen roof, and the great Gold Dust Dagoba, which protected sacred relics. Shaped like a giant bell, the latter was strewn with thousands of bright flowers, the gifts of worshipers.

Leaving Anuradhapura, the brothers went on a way that took them north and west towards the shore of the sea. Never, they thought as they rode along, had Serendip seemed more serene, never more beautiful. In the morning, sunlight fell on the red and yellow blossoms of tall flame trees that grew on either side of the way. At night, moonflowers opened, and the air was fragrant with jasmine.

Balakrama rejoiced in beholding clusters of white dove orchids, which, like the flights of small birds, could be seen here and there in the forests. Vijayo stopped to listen to the songs and stories of boys and girls, while Rajahsingha conversed with all the officials he happened to meet along the way and inquired about their villages.

But each of the travelers, as he rode, said in silence to himself: "How can we find a single scroll lost in the great world, and when again shall I see my beloved country?"

One afternoon as they neared the sea, the princes were tired and thirsty. For a moment's rest, they stopped at a farmhouse nestling near a great tank. Here, standing in a rice field beside a grove of palu trees, was a young girl. Her eyes were on the small plants at her feet, and she held a bunch of flowers in her hand.

As the three brothers halted, the oldest spoke.

"We are travelers," he said, "weary from a long ride and very thirsty. Will you give us some water to drink?"

The girl raised her eyes. When Balakrama looked into them, his heart was filled with joy and trembling. This farmer's daughter was as graceful as the jasmine vine and fairer than any lady he had ever seen.

His joy soon disappeared, however, because while he and his brothers waited for her to bring them water, he remembered that he must leave the country without delay. So he trembled once more, this time with fear that he might never see her again.

Then, accepting the water she brought him, the oldest prince learned that her name was Podihamine and that she lived in this place with her father and her mother. After a few moments, he spoke words of thanks and offered the young woman some gold for her trouble, but she would not touch it.

Tucking blossoms of white jasmine in her dark hair and giving him a smile, which seemed to Balakrama as sweet as the song of a mountain bird, she bade farewell. So, sadly and in obedience to the king's decree, the oldest prince departed with his brothers.

At last the young men reached the coast. Here they arranged for some mahouts to return with their elephants to Anuradhapura. The brothers, themselves, boarded a small ship to cross the strait to India; but each looked longingly at the shore they were leaving, especially Balakrama. As the vessel pulled away, he sang of Podihamine; and with this song, the three princes sailed away from Serendip:

PANTOUM FOR PODIHAMINE

As she weaves white jasmine in her hair
Before we leave the isle by ship,
Podihamine is smiling there
To charm the sons of Serendip.

Before we leave the isle by ship,
A bulbul sings in a palu tree
To charm the sons of Serendip,
And nestles in our memory.

A bulbul sings in a palu tree;
Podihamine is smiling there
And nestles in our memory
As she weaves white jasmine in her hair.

THE
Lost Camel

The three princes slipped away from Serendip on a bright and singing day. Before their ship was far from land, however, gray clouds were marching overhead, and sharp winds whipped the sea into furious billows.

Between the surging peaks, the three young men saw dark and threatening shapes, monstrous heads and lashing tails. With tremendous force, these struck against the small vessel. It tossed from side to side, now up, now down, then nearly over.

But the three brothers showed no fear. They took long oars and with these tried to strike down the ugly dragons in the sea. Every blow, however, fell only into yielding foam. The scaly monsters still leapt and dodged among the waves.

"Death to Dragons," said Balakrama, a little out of breath, "we must find as soon as possible."

His brothers agreed. Therefore, once arrived on land and having purchased horses, the princes made haste to visit all the learned men they could find. Some of these, so aged they could barely smile, just put a finger to their lips and shook their heads. Others pondered aloud, but gave no real answer.

Then one night as the brothers rode through the high lands of the Cheras, they came to a village where they learned of an old and noted sage. They asked the way to his house, and a group of men and children brought them directly to the philosopher's doorway. Here he sat as still as sleep, and yet his eyes were open.

The brothers, dismounting from their horses, bowed with great respect.

"Pray, tell us," Balakrama said, "if from your wisdom's store you can furnish us with an old lost formula, by ancients known as *Death to Dragons?*"

At these words, the sage looked up and said, "A hundred lines it has, but there is one and only one lone copy of the total formula in all the world."

Feeling his heart dance within him, Balakrama said quickly, "And where, pray, may that be?"

"Who knows? Alas," the philosopher replied, "it is possessed by a strange and ancient seer with eyes that dart like sudden flame. By some he is called Aphoenicius. So closely does he guard the scroll on which the formula is written, that he travels in a hundred guises, at times invisible. Rarely does he stay more than one day and night in a single place.

"As for the verses, it is said that these are carried in a cylinder of silver closed tightly at both ends. Many kings have tried to buy its contents, but to all who ask Aphoenicius will only say, '*Death to Dragons* may not be sold. *Death to Dragons* may not be bought.' "

"But you," Balakrama said, "have you ever looked upon the seer yourself?"

"I have," the sage replied. "Once, long before the moon grew old, he came this way and stopped a single night beneath my roof. Well I knew the fabled scroll was somewhere hidden on his person, but dared not ask to see it."

Then suddenly, the philosopher looked hard at the princes.

"And why do you three," he said in a stern voice, "ask about this magic thing?"

The brothers explained that they sought to rid the sea around their island home of monstrous dragons. At this the old man waved away the other people and invited the three princes to step into his house.

There he spoke in a voice barely above a whisper.

"Although I never saw even the cylinder of silver, the night that Aphoenicius rested here, I heard him saying verses in his sleep. Only two lines were said distinctly, but these I noted down."

He opened a small cabinet and took therefrom some old dried leaves of the talipot palm. On one of these was written:

"Though the treasure saline be,
You will not scoop it from the sea."

Hastily Balakrama made a copy of these two lines. Then the three brothers thanked the gentle sage and continued on their way, wondering more than ever how the formula could be secured.

One morning shortly after, as they traveled slowly toward the north and west, the princes were overtaken by a messenger from Serendip.

"What news? What news?" asked all of them at once.

"Your Highnesses," the man replied, bowing very respectfully, "I regret to bear you word that our noble king has fallen ill."

The brothers were distressed and much alarmed. They longed to go back to Serendip at once; but, alas, they had no permission to return. So Balakrama composed a letter to be taken to King Jaiya.

In it the princes told of their sorrow at his illness. Then recounting all that had happened, they sent him the two strange lines of verse which they had found.

"Since the rest is so closely guarded," the letter said, "and even were it found, cannot be purchased, we entreat Your Majesty to let us now return to Serendip. There we could drive the dragons from our shores with shining swords."

Afterwards, though hopeful that they soon would journey home, the three young men set out once more upon their search. They traveled slowly and the sun rose and set for many days and many nights and then at last they came to the land of Persia. A vast country of both deserts and mountains, it was ruled by a powerful emperor whose name was Vahram.

Near its borders, the brothers sold the horses upon which they had been traveling. In their place they purchased camels for the journey which lay ahead across the desert. Mounted upon these, they set out for the imperial capital at Bishapur.

One morning in the desert they noticed great streaks of dried salt glistening in the sunlight, left behind perhaps by some long-gone ocean. Balakrama thought of the two lines of verse.

"Here is salt not in the sea but on the land," he said. "Can this be what the verses speak of?" His brothers could not tell.

Traveling still farther, they saw here and there trees of wild pistachio with old and twisted trunks, and in time the foothills of a lofty mountain range. The sharp eyes of Balakrama, however, noted small things, too. Near the mountain streams he saw grass growing along the way and in the dust, prints made by the plodding feet of men and beasts traveling before them.

One morning, the princes reached the province of ancient Fars and left the desert. At once they purchased horses, leaving behind their camels to be bought by others going towards the east.

Now the brothers could travel more swiftly, and before long they spied a mountain village far off. Even at a distance, however, they could see the dome of its temple of fire, and to the west beyond the houses, plowed fields, where farmers seemed hard at work.

About the same time they overtook a small caravan

which had halted on the road. In the midst of it a stocky camel leader in a brown and tattered tunic was asking questions and shouting orders.

"I can see you are exceedingly busy," Balakrama said to him, "but pray, tell me if you know the name of the village which lies ahead."

The man replied with few words.

"Kuhabad," he said. "People mostly poor, but kind to strangers."

He seemed to have something else on his mind. Turning from the princes, he asked more questions and gave commands in a sharp voice. Then he began to wring his hands and spoke again to the three brothers.

"Worthy Gentlemen," he said, perhaps taking them for merchants, "have you seen a wandering camel? One is missing from our number. We looked ahead. We looked behind. No camel."

He flung out his hands.

"Many caravans have we passed," Balakrama said, "but we have not seen a camel separated from his fellows. A long way back, however, I observed the footprints of such a creature. He was headed towards the east on a path but little traveled. Tell us, did yours lack the sight of one eye?"

"Why, that he did," the leader said in amazement. "For a whole year he has seen with only one."

"And had he also lost a tooth?" the oldest prince inquired.

"Indeed, he had!" answered the leader, his voice sounding more astonished than before. Then apparently in too great haste even to thank Balakrama, he turned back to look again.

For their part, the princes continued on toward the west. Their path lay upward between grassy slopes, where wild tulips with blossoms of red and white swayed in the breeze. The time passed swiftly, and soon the three young men reached Kuhabad.

Around it were farmlands where the villagers grew their food, and the princes saw young wheat plants which had pushed through the dark earth. The houses were made with bricks of hardened mud; and passing near the temple, which they had glimpsed from a distance, the brothers saw a sacred fire burning within.

Between the houses of Kuhabad ran narrow pathways to its center, where there was a small open space with a spring of water. Here blossoms of apricot and quince trees spilled their fragrance in the air.

The princes had decided to ask in this village if anyone knew of Aphoenicius and his scroll. But they had arrived just as the celebration of a wedding was going forward, and the father of the bridegroom invited them to share in the happiness of the day. They had hardly begun to enjoy the company and to taste the feast of mutton, sweet melons and rice, however, when the camel leader, bristling with rage, burst in upon them.

"Look you," he said to the princes, "I have not found my camel, nor any sign of him." His dark eyes flashed with anger. "Why did you send me on an empty errand? You have played a wicked joke."

Balakrama said, "I regret that you have not found

the animal you seek, but I do truly believe I saw his traces. Was he not halt in one leg?"

"That he was. That he was," the leader said, again wringing his hands. "You describe my beast exactly."

Then his eyes narrowed, and he spoke harsh words. "Since you know so much, you must have stolen him. Say quickly where he is, or I shall tell the emperor's guards. They will bring you to justice."

When the princes protested that they had not taken nor even seen the camel, the leader rent the air with his fury. Not wanting to occasion further disturbance at the wedding, the three princes decided to proceed at once to Bishapur.

Riding swiftly, they soon reached the imperial capital. Situated in a fair valley where date trees grew, it had straight streets, a high-domed temple for its sacred fire, and a great palace.

As soon as possible after they had arrived, the brothers set out to examine the magnificence all around; but they had little opportunity to do so. For they were just approaching the town's center for the first time, when suddenly an armed band of the emperor's guard blocked their way on every side.

"Here are those camel robbers," its commander shouted. "In the name of the Mighty Emperor Vahram, you shall go no farther."

"But this is monstrous," Balakrama said. "I tried to help—"

"Silence!" the commander roared.

Without being allowed even one more word, the three princes were arrested and taken off to a military

there was a large crowd following and jeering at the three young men.

It was at this time that an old woman turned her eyes upward and silently prayed for the triumph of good over evil. Doing so, she was surprised to see a strange bird with wings of gold and eyes like fire. Swooping through the sky, it dipped low for just an instant and then was gone.

No one else saw it. The people were watching the procession of the three brothers surrounded by the imperial guards.

The princes had almost reached the garrison when suddenly a man who was a neighbor of the camel leader appeared around a corner urging along the lost animal. He had found and recognized the creature, straying towards the east just as Prince Balakrama had supposed.

With this news, the people in the crowd slunk away like shadows. The camel leader was almost overcome with amazement. For a moment he could not even express his joy at seeing the camel again. Then, being an honest man, he was determined to undo the wrong he had done. Hastily he ran to the imperial palace. Here he sent word to the emperor concerning what had happened and requested the immediate release of the three wronged men.

Vahram, already struck by the noble bearing and courteous behavior of the brothers, was now more impressed than ever and was delighted that the men were innocent. He sent for them at once.

When the three princes appeared, he said, "I am

garrison. Here, bound with chains, they were thrust into a damp and somber prison.

When the story of the stolen camel reached the emperor, he was far from pleased; he had always taken special care for the safety of the imperial highways. Learning that the three strangers were young and carried themselves with courtesy, he decided to hear the case himself.

So the brothers were taken out of prison and brought suddenly into an open court in a main square of the city. Here they saw throngs of people, both young and old, all anxious to see the captives and hear the trial.

The emperor, himself, arrived riding upon a lively horse and accompanied by a great train of officials. His dark hair was nearly covered by a cap which glistened with sapphires, and his young face was stern but handsome. Below his neatly waved moustache, the tip of his short and curly beard was ornamented with a single ruby, superb in brilliance. He wore a coat of bright blue, and his white silken trousers were draped in a multitude of folds.

Also in the open square the three brothers saw their accuser, the leader of camels. This man when permitted to speak, bowed and said excitedly to the emperor, "O Noble and Imperial Majesty, before you is a wicked man. He described my lost camel exactly: his eye, his mouth, and his leg! Clearly, he and those with him must have stolen my valuable beast. I beg you for justice."

Thereupon, Vahram turned to the oldest prince and said, "Did you speak as this man has said?"

Balakrama bowed and replied, "Your Imperial esty, I did."

Before he could say more, the emperor declared the three brothers must indeed be guilty.

"It is plain that you merit a punishment of th verest kind," he said to them sternly, "but I shall with clemency to spare your lives if you will im diately return to this poor man the camel you h stolen."

Although threatened with death, the three prin showed no sign of fear.

Instead, Balakrama bowed very low before the e peror and said, "O Ruler of Mighty Kings, we a three young men who travel to behold the wonders a customs of the world. Hither we came eager to obser all the marvels of your great dominions.

"None of us has seen this leader's camel, and on because of careful reasoning did we suppose the cre ture to be as I described. Pray, let the leader searc again, and if our words are found untrue, then punis us in any way your wisdom may devise."

"Enough," the emperor said. "It is not to be be lieved that you are magicians. Yet your description wa in all points exact. Therefore, I say that you must hav stolen the camel, and you must die unless it is returned."

The guards seized the unfortunate princes, still bound with chains, and thrust them along the streets to return by foot to prison. Swaggering ahead of them, the camel leader called out his news to all he saw. Soon

wonderfully eager to hear your reasoning in this matter. Tell me," he said, turning to Balakrama, "how you discovered without seeing the animal that he was blind in one eye?"

"O King Over Many Kings," the oldest prince replied, bowing very respectfully, "this I supposed because on only the left side of the road had the grass been nibbled, even though it was taller and greener on the other."

Vahram slapped his sides with pleasure. "Well-observed and well-reasoned," he said. "But how were you able to conclude that he also lacked a single tooth?"

"O Mighty Monarch and Pride of Many Peoples," Balakrama replied, "it seemed clear to me that one of his teeth must indeed be gone, for scattered along your imperial way were bits of grass only partly chewed, and those pieces were no larger than could have slipped from a camel's mouth where a tooth was missing."

At this, the emperor's eyes opened wide with delight, and he was eager to hear the rest.

"Now, pray, by what signs," he said, "did you also conjecture that this wretched beast was halt in one leg?"

"O Powerful Ruler and Noble Emperor," Balakrama said, "this I judged by marks left in the way, for it seemed that one leg had been dragged along the ground."

At this Vahram laughed aloud, rejoicing in the cleverness of Balakrama. Wishing to show all three brothers marks of special kindness in view of the severe judgment he had earlier meted out to them, with no further delay he invited them to visit in his palace.

The imperial residence had high imposing domes, and on the outside were figures of great kings sculptured in stone. At its entrance were lofty arches, and its hall of state had silvered columns and a floor with mosaic designs depicting many people from famous stories.

The three princes were welcomed into sumptuous quarters which opened on a court adorned with a fountain and flowering garden. Inside, the walls of their rooms bore designs of lions and wild boars incised in the plaster, and hangings made of woven wool. Here Vahram not only entertained the brothers like kings, but was so charmed by their conversation that he let no day pass without coming to visit them.

As royal guests, the princes were well-pleased with the fortunate outcome of their camel adventure. But soon they were far from happy at news which reached them from Serendip.

"How is His Majesty the King?" they asked the messenger who arrived with a letter.

Bowing respectfully to the royal brothers before replying, he said, "It is my grievous duty to inform you that His Majesty daily grows worse rather than better; and since he cannot travel about as he was used to do, the officers in charge of our great tanks grow fat and slothful."

"Then perhaps he summons us home," said Balakrama, hastily opening his father's message.

Two lines alone from an ancient formula are useless, the letter from Jaiya said. *Moreover, swords cannot beat down the fierce dragons that plague our shores.*

So even though my head grows weary, I find no suitable reason to call you home.

Deeply struck with disappointment, Balakrama had a letter written to Jaiya explaining how impossible it seemed ever to find a single scroll carried by one who could travel in a hundred guises. He urged the king to allow his sons to return at once: *Let us help you to watch over the great tanks and attack the dragons of the sea with mighty spears.*

Finally, the oldest of the princes told of their adventure concerning the camel and how, unexpectedly, a powerful emperor had become their friend.

"When our father reads this," Balakrama said, "it will gladden his heart. Surely then he will give us permission to return to Serendip."

Hopeful once more, the three princes rejoiced in the kindness that had been shown them not only in a palace of Bishapur but in the small village of Kuhabad. So they made this song:

PANTOUM FOR THE PEOPLE OF KUHABAD

The villagers walk close to stars
While the mountain tulips sway,
Kissed by winds of ancient Fars,
On a Persian wedding day.

While the mountain tulips sway
A bridegroom marries his gentle bride
On a Persian wedding day
In Kuhabad, where princes ride.

A bridegroom marries his gentle bride,
Kissed by winds of ancient Fars.
In Kuhabad, where princes ride,
The villagers walk close to stars.

THE

Ugly Plot

Not long after the princes first arrived in the imperial palace of the Emperor Vahram, on a day when spring had nudged the peach trees into bloom, Vijayo awoke to the sound of a young girl's voice. So sweetly was it raised in song, the very morning seemed to hear each tender note.

The second prince was charmed to such a degree, that he felt that he must hear at least once more the enchanting singer. In those distant days, however, politeness forbade him, as a guest and stranger, to ask her name. Therefore, with a gallant effort he tried to content himself by hoping that someone would speak it in his presence or that he might hear her voice again.

As for the emperor, he continued every day to visit the princes. This being so, they early took occasion to ask if he had any knowledge of the powerful potion which ancients knew as *Death to Dragons.*

"Very little," said Vahram, "except that a poor mad seer called Aphoenicius claims to own its formula, written on a scroll and carried everywhere with him in a cylinder of silver. Once, when he came this way, Zahmes, my Grand Keeper of the Royal Orders, asked its price.

" '*Death to Dragons* cannot be sold. *Death to Dragons* cannot be bought,' was all the old man said."

Vahram raised his dark brows.

"But why do you inquire about this matter?" he asked.

"Because," Vijayo said, "around our home the seas are sorely plagued by dragons, and these may be vanquished only with a powerful magic."

Finding his guests deeply concerned, the emperor said he would have his learned scholars consulted at once. In the meantime, the brothers were invited to attend his imperial court. At this it was Vahram's custom to hear petitions of the highest ranking subjects of his empire.

On the appointed day, the three princes and all the nobles of the capital gathered in the great hall of silvered columns. Here twenty-one musicians played upon harps, and the emperor, seated on a throne of gold, wore a crimson robe embroidered with rubies and pearls in designs of crescents and peacocks. Exactly over his head, hung by a glistening chain from the high-domed ceiling, was a crown of jewels and precious metal.

Looking about them, the princes saw a vassal king, who, they were told, formerly ruled one of the largest provinces of the land. With a great retinue of his officers, he had come to plead before the emperor.

When permitted to speak, he said, "O, Mighty Ruler of Many Peoples, I have come to beg clemency for my son. Pray, revoke the dreadful sentence of banishment which you laid upon him."

"It appears," Vahram said, "that you govern your son no better than your kingdom, which belongs to our empire. I have had to keep you nearby as a royal hostage for the good behavior of your people. With your son, however, it is different. Once trusted as an officer of the Imperial Treasury, he has himself admitted to stealing both bronze and gold for his own dark purposes. Therefore, he shall not step upon this land again lest his wrongdoings multiply and spread across our domain like a foul plague."

At these words, the face of the vassal king flushed and seemed to draw in upon itself. Speaking in a voice so low that in all the court only Vijayo with his sharp ears and those very close could hear him, the vassal king asked for water to drink. He left the hall with head held low.

The same morning the three brothers discussed among themselves the scene that they had witnessed.

"Even though his son was pronounced guilty of serious crimes," Vijayo said, "I could easily sense from his voice that the royal hostage harbored some plan of dark revenge. We must warn the Emperor in order that he may thwart any plot against his life."

That day Vahram came to visit the brothers as usual. After all of them had jumped up quickly and bowed with deep respect, the second prince said, "Your Imperial Majesty, our hearts are filled with apprehension for your safety. Indeed, I fear that even now your precious life may be in danger."

"How can this be?" the emperor said. "Unfold your thinking to me, for it does not seem possible that such can be the case. And yet I hesitate to doubt your wisdom."

"While your Majesty spoke to the hostage," Vijayo said, "I could hear implacable anger storming through his heart. Besides, he called for water to drink, which I take as a sign of the fiery rage boiling deep within him."

Vahram said, "Can this be so? It can hardly be supposed that a petty vassal would dare to plan a crime against the imperial throne of Persia. Besides, in spite of my decision this morning, he has invited me and all my court to attend a feast in the palace where I permit him to live."

"O Noble Emperor," Vijayo said, "could it not be that he did so with an evil purpose? I beg Your Imperial Majesty to exercise the greatest caution before going as a guest to his residence."

When the emperor saw that all three of the princes were of similar mind, he asked Vijayo what steps they would recommend.

The second prince replied, "Could we not summon to these quarters some humble member of your vassal's household? Thus very quietly, inquiries may be made concerning any special preparations for the feast."

Now in those days, it was not usual for a great emperor to speak directly to a man who was neither an official nor a member of the nobility; but in this matter, so closely touching his own life, Vahram decided to do so, and agreed to Vijayo's plan. Very secretly it was carried out.

The second prince sent for a young cook in the household of the petty king. When he arrived the next day and the princes brought him before the emperor, the poor man trembled with fear and fell on his knees before the ruler.

"You have nothing to fear," Vahram said, "if you speak the truth. Now tell me, is any special delicacy being prepared for me and for me alone in the palace of my royal hostage?"

"Your Imperial Majesty," the young man said, "I have been told that at the end of the great feast, he will give to you and to you alone a certain drink. It will be in a goblet of crystal and be brought to you upon a golden dish carved with the design of a wild boar."

Here he stopped speaking as if he were afraid to say any more.

"Yes, yes," the emperor said. "What of that? Speak up."

"One day . . . one day, Sir," the cook continued, "an

old man with flashing eyes, but dressed as a beggar, came asking for food at the door of our kitchen. I was filled with pity, let him slip inside, and gave him soup, Sir, with rice."

"What happened then?" Vahram asked.

"He had finished this, Sir, and was about to fall asleep when he saw the goblet of crystal. At this, Sir, he suddenly sat up straight and said, 'Whom, may I ask, will be served with this?'

" 'His Majesty the Emperor,' I said. 'Is it not beautiful?'

" 'Treachery,' he said then, 'treachery, treachery,' and fell asleep."

"What thought you of this?" Vahram said.

"Hearing his words, Sir, and knowing how the king grieves over his son's disgrace," the young man went on, "I could not escape a fear that the drink might be poisoned."

The emperor's eyes opened wide with amazement, and he motioned for Vijayo to ask further questions.

"What else did the old man say?" the second prince inquired.

"No more," the young man said, "except that as he rested on a chair in our kitchen, he dozed a little and muttered verses in his sleep. Only a few words, though, did he say plainly."

Vijayo caught his breath and glanced quickly at his brothers. Then he spoke to the man.

"What were those?" he asked.

Very slowly, as if wondering what they meant, the cook repeated them:

"And often from the sight is hidden
Such magic not by wishes bidden."

Vijayo repeated the lines so that he would not forget them before they were written down.

"Sir," he said to the emperor, "these verses are so like the others which we heard, that I cannot but believe that they were spoken by Aphoenicius disguised as a beggar. For this reason, though he seemed just a poor wanderer, I entreat you not to disregard his words."

Then Vijayo turned back to the young man. "And where is the beggar now?" he said.

"I turned to stir the soup," the cook replied, "and when I looked back, he was gone."

Vahram's eyes shone with amazement as if he could hardly believe the words he just had heard. Then commanding the cook to speak to no one of his visit to the palace, he gave him a bag of coins and dismissed him with thanks.

As soon as the young man had gone, the emperor poured out his gratitude to the princes and especially to Vijayo. Also he offered to let the princes lead a search for the missing seer. This offer the brothers accepted eagerly.

For a day and a night, the princes and a host of the emperor's guards, riding in ever-widening circles around the capital, sought the old man; but no one of his description did they find. Then, knowing that Aphoenicius might appear in any of a hundred guises and could also make himself invisible, the princes decided that further searching in this way was useless.

So they rode back to the palace and turned their attention to the matter of protecting the emperor. On this he soon consulted with them.

"Since you ask our counsel, and because we have the deepest concern for your safety," Vijayo said, "I shall say there seems but one course to follow. Attend the feast to which you have been asked, but when the goblet is presented, invite the vassal king to drink therefrom, himself. If he does so, you will know that he is innocent; if he refuses, it may well be supposed that he is guilty."

Before long, the day of the feast arrived. The three princes rose early and prepared to accompany the emperor.

When they were all on the point of departing, it happened that once more Vijayo heard a young woman's voice pouring forth a song of unutterable sweetness. Each note smote deeply the heart of the young prince.

Doubting not that the singer was the same he had heard before, Vijayo was loath to leave the palace until suddenly he realized that the song, long-ended, was sounding only in his heart. He turned about and made haste to rejoin the imperial party.

After riding through land rich in wheat fields and date trees, they arrived at the residence of the royal hostage. The emperor was received with the sound of three and thirty trumpets, and the princes saw their host give him a golden ring set with opals and onyx.

Then while musicians played, Vahram was served

his favorite dish, a sweet pilau of finest rice with saffron and tangerines.

When the repast was nearly ended, the vassal king, himself, brought forth a special drink in a goblet of crystal which rested upon a golden dish bearing the design of a wild boar.

"This," he said to the emperor, "is a most exquisite and valuable refreshment, prepared especially for you. Among other virtues, it cools the liver, sweetens the tongue, and drives all anger from the heart. I pray you, taste and enjoy it, Your Majesty."

Vahram looked upon the goblet which had been described to him by the young cook. There was no need to question what the brew contained. He said to the royal vassal, "If this drink has such extraordinary properties, surely you have more reason to need it than I. It seems to me quite possible, that some bitterness may still be camping in your heart. Therefore, I command you now and in my presence to drink from this goblet yourself."

"Heaven forbid that I should taste of so rare a delicacy," said the vassal king. "It is fit only for a mighty ruler who, like yourself, is the delight and sovereign of an empire."

"However agreeable and useful this drink may be," Vahram said, "my order remains unchanged. You, not I, shall now partake of its special qualities."

Thereupon the royal hostage fell on his knees before the emperor. His voice as he spoke was filled with fear.

"Alas," he said, "now have I fallen into the misfortune I had planned for you! I can only hope you

will consider the distress of a father's heart, and that your mercy will exceed your severity."

The emperor spoke quietly.

"O petty king and base vassal," he said, "for so enormous a crime, I could have you executed in an instant. But, though I possess no sons of my own, I think I can understand how the loss of one, even though wicked, may distress a grieving father. Therefore, I shall be merciful and let you live; but like your son, you shall be banished forever from this empire."

Later, when Vahram had returned to his palace, he summoned the three princes and said, "You have served me well, and I thank you with a grateful heart. Upon each of you, I bestow a robe adorned with gold and pearls and one of my finest horses. As for you," he said to Vijayo, "since it was your sharp ears that first surmised my vassal's plot, I invite you to come to me in three days and ask for what you will. If the fulfillment of your wish lies within my power, it shall be granted."

Now on the morning when the three days came to an end, an old man on a nearby farm rose early because he could not sleep. Standing at the entrance of his rustic house, he raised his eyes to watch a wild hare as it leapt up the steep sides of a mountain.

Then abruptly the farmer noticed a strange bird. It had golden wings and eyes like fiery stars. Darting out of the sky for an instant, the bird dipped low over the emperor's palace. Finally it disappeared behind a rosy cloud. The people in the old man's family did not see it, for all of them were still asleep.

A little later the same day, as the second prince was making ready to appear before the emperor, he was suddenly aware of the singer he had heard before. Her silvery voice rose like a delicate fountain, and each note subsided as the softest spray in a summer's twilight. At that moment, the young man yearned more than ever to know her name and see her face.

A few minutes later he stood with his brothers before the emperor.

Vahram said to the second prince, "My gratitude to you for saving my life is like an overflowing pool. Pray, tell me what you wish."

Vijayo hesitated just a moment. Then calling upon all the courtesy that had been taught him, he said, "Your Imperial Majesty has already shown to me and to my brothers so much kindness that I hope you will permit us to serve you in some useful way."

Vahram said, "Your generous wish shall soon be granted."

Then he smiled and continued, "Since you have wanted to keep your origin a secret, hospitality does not permit me to ask it. Nevertheless, I perceive by your courtesy and bearing that you surely come of noble station. Moreover, you have saved my life. Hence, it is my pleasure to bestow upon you the hand of my only sister in marriage. Let the Princess Purandocht come forth."

He signaled to a servant, who drew a curtain. From behind it came a royal lady fairer than a Persian rose. She had dark hair, shining eyes, and wore a robe of violet silk, embroidered with pearls. Moreover as soon as she spoke a few words, Vijayo recognized her voice as the one that he had heard in song.

When the joyous prince could at last express his gratitude and happiness, he said, "Your Imperial Majesty does too much kindness to your humble friend. While obedience to my father requires that I first seek his consent upon my marriage, I assure you no prospect could be more agreeable to my heart if the royal lady also finds herself content."

At these words, the Princess Purandocht cast down her eyes and said, "It would be enough just to obey my noble brother, but since he has chosen for me one to whom he owes his very life and whose love of songs and stories is like my own, the gratitude and happiness of my heart must overflow."

The three princes were delighted at the thought of so felicitous and high-placed an alliance. So each in turn expressed his pleasure.

Vahram thanked them all again for their help in thwarting the plot of the vassal king. Then he went on to talk with them gravely about a further difficulty.

"Formerly in this country evil arose less often than nowadays," he said, "because my grandfather possessed a device called the Mirror of Justice, which had been found by philosophers of ancient times. This glass, inherited by my father and uncle, had the property of reflecting both truth and falsehood.

"When two people were at difference, both were obliged to look into it. As they did so, the face of the one who had lied, immediately turned purple. The face of the one in the right, retained its own color; and so the latter one would win his case."

"And the loser," asked the youngest prince, Rajahsingha, "what happened to him?"

"Such a one did not regain his proper complexion," Vahram said, "until he had been lowered into a deep pit, there to live on bread and water for thirty-seven days. Afterwards, if he confessed his falsehood, his own proper color returned and he was raised back up again."

"That was certainly a wondrous mirror," said the third prince, thinking how great an aid to any ruler would be a device so remarkable.

"As you can well imagine," the emperor continued, "people lived in fear of its strange power. They kept their behavior in bounds, and the land was tranquil and happy."

"But where is the glass now?" said Rajahsingha.

"Alas," the emperor replied, "it was taken away by my uncle and given to the young queen of a country in India. She will not return it to us, for this marvelous mirror saves her land from a sore affliction."

Then he showed the princes a letter received from his uncle in India.

Often, it said, *one can see hovering in the air over the capital city here, a great right hand with fingers extended. It stays in the sky either a long or a short time, then suddenly swoops downward. In former years, whenever this happened, it would seize a man and cast him into the ocean. Now, however, the queen, whose name is Parvathi, has the Mirror of Justice brought out to reflect the hand, whereat, without taking any of her people, it sinks back into the sea.*

"A strange matter, indeed," Rajahsingha said. "One can clearly see why Her Majesty is loath to part with so marvelous a glass."

Vahram said, "Even though I have offered her jeweled rings, three thousand pounds of silk brocade, and the fleetest horses in the world, she could not be persuaded to part with the mirror. Indeed, I am convinced that never will she do so unless some other way can be found to free her kingdom from the scourge of the Fearsome Hand."

The emperor was silent for a moment, then said, "From what I have already observed of your abilities, gentlemen, I am persuaded that you may be able to conquer the Hand and so restore the Mirror of Justice to us. Also," he said, turning to Vijayo, "mindful of the wish you expressed to me this morning, I venture to ask you and your brothers to undertake the task."

Speaking for all the princes, Vijayo said, "We are grateful for the high esteem your words convey and for your many kindnesses. Therefore, on the splendid horses you have given us, we shall ride into India and do all that we can to serve you in this matter."

The emperor was overjoyed at his words. He thanked each of the young princes and entrusted to them rich and delicate gifts for the great Queen Parvathi.

On the same day, the brothers received another letter from their father and asked questions of its bearer.

"How is His Majesty, and how fares our country?"

Bowing deeply, the messenger replied, "Your Royal Highnesses, to both your questions, I must answer 'ill indeed.' His Majesty's health has not improved, and the great tanks are so neglected that already the waters in them are dangerously low."

"Then perhaps our father invites us to return," Vijayo said, opening the letter; but he read:

Balakrama was clever to describe a camel he had not seen, and it is advantageous for my sons to win the friendship of an emperor, but the dragons off our shores cannot be vanquished with mighty spears, and nothing I have so far heard persuades me that you are ready to be rulers or that I should call you home.

Deeply disappointed again, the three princes took counsel together, and this time, it was Vijayo who composed a letter to King Jaiya. In it, the three brothers sent word of their sorrow at his continued illness and begged to return home so that they might help him protect the great reservoirs.

Also, having included the two more lines they had found, they told of their fruitless search for Aphoenicius. *Not only does he travel disguised, but can, it seems, make himself invisible. How then shall we ever find him and the rest of the formula? Instead of searching farther, pray, let us come back to our homeland and fight the fierce dragons with swift arrows.*

Finally, the letter told of the thwarted plot against the emperor's life, and of how in gratitude, Vahram had offered his sister in marriage to Vijayo.

"When His Majesty reads this," the second prince said, "surely he will be delighted and allow his sons to breathe once more the fragrant air of Serendip."

So, full of hope, the three brothers made ready to

travel into India. Before they did so, however, they made this new and serious song:

PANTOUM FOR A PETTY KING

O hollow hospitality!
Not knowing all had been foreknown,
As the vassal stoops to treachery,
He soon must lose his silver throne.

Not knowing all had been foreknown
This petty king fails in his plot.
He soon must lose his silver throne,
And banishment becomes his lot.

This petty king fails in his plot
As the vassal stoops to treachery,
And banishment becomes his lot.
O hollow hospitality!

THE

Sorry Quarrel

Early one morning, the three princes waited upon the emperor in the great hall of silvered columns in order to take their leave.

"My noble friends," the emperor said, "your coming to say farewell is indeed courteous. But since it is for us you are setting forth, I myself shall accompany you as far as Kuhabad. Thus, if only for a little time, we may postpone farewells."

Therefore, Vahram with a host of officers and other nobles in his suite, mounted his charger and accompanied the princes as far as the mountain village where once, not long before, the three brothers had been guests at a wedding. Here, while men and women, boys and girls, eagerly sought a glimpse of the emperor's party, musicians on their harps and flutes played tunes of parting. Then Vahram bade adieu to the three young men.

"My heart goes with you on your daring essay against the Fearsome Hand," he said. "And I look hopefully for your return."

The youngest brother, Rajahsingha, replied with equal courtesy. "Sir, if in venturing thus, we may in some small measure be of service to you, it will be to our joy and high delight."

After every farewell had been said, the emperor watched the departure of the three brothers until at last they disappeared around a sudden curve of the mountain road. Then he rode about to see the farms and houses of his people in this place, and to learn if they were well and happy.

Vahram watched the farmers cutting hay for their animals and storing it close to their homes in the village. He also admired the handiwork of the women whose woven baskets, rugs, and shawls were displayed in the market place. And finally, he reached the temple with its brilliant fire, which burned by day and by night. Here he dismounted, and before returning to Bishapur, prayed for the success of the three young men who had just set out for India.

It was later, while the emperor was returning to the capital, that the imperial party overtook an especially large caravan of traders. They were riding upon camels with bells that could be heard a long way off.

Having sent Zahmes, his Grand Keeper of the Royal Orders, to make inquiries of the merchant in charge, Vahram learned that the travelers came from the distant East, bringing with them a great number of rare and curious treasures. Since he delighted in all that was strange and elegant, the emperor asked that these articles be conveyed into the courtyard of the palace, where in comfort he might inspect them.

Soon, therefore, he repaired thither with his courtiers to see what the caravan had brought. As the bright and colorful objects were spread out, Vahram was delighted. He saw bowls shaped like delicate flowers, velvets as fine as the down on butterfly wings, and ornaments which sparkled like sunshine dancing on a mountain lake.

Yet all of these seemed plain and of little worth after he had observed the beauty of a young woman who appeared for a few moments in the courtyard and spoke to the merchant. He saw that she was slender and lithe as a young peach tree. Her hair, falling to her shoulders, shone like polished jet. Her eyes, in the shape of almonds, were as dark as a mine of rarest gems, and her lips seemed like fragments of a rosy cloud.

The emperor was so enchanted with this lovely being that he asked Zahmes to find out all he could about her.

"She is called Deliramma," this officer reported, "but the leader of the caravan can say little of her origin save that he found her as an infant, near a forest of a distant kingdom in the land of India. He has since

taken care of her as a foster father."

When Vahram heard this, he commanded the merchant to be brought before him and inquired more closely into the matter.

"Your Imperial Majesty," the man said, bowing low, "although I have asked my questions everywhere, nowhere have I found an answer to the mystery. My conjecture, Sir, is that she was stolen for ransom and that the abductors lost their courage and abandoned the child at the edge of the forest. There, traveling along, I happened to find her."

"If ransom was the original object," Vahram said, "surely she belonged to a family of more than humble station. How was she clothed when first you saw her?"

"That I can more easily show than tell," the merchant said.

He opened a box and brought forth a length of silk, soft blue in color.

"With this the child was clothed," he said.

Then he clapped, and the young woman appeared again. Taking her by the hand, he led her before the emperor and showed Vahram a chain of tiny links in the shape of crowns, which she wore around her arm.

"When I found her as an infant," said the merchant, "she was wearing this as a necklace. Now, too small for that purpose, it serves as a bracelet."

"I cannot guess whose daughter she is," the emperor said, "but that these were the belongings of an infant nobly born, I have no doubt."

"With this, Your Imperial Majesty, I can only agree," the foster father said, "but when I found the child, she was too young to speak, nor growing up, could she remember aught to tell us of her past. Only the tunes she sings suggest she may have heard in her former days some songs we never knew."

The emperor then desired that she be asked to sing. To this she readily consented, and so melodious was her voice, so artless her manner, that Vahram was moved to offer her the protection of his own household. This he told her foster father.

For a few moments, the merchant was silent.

The emperor, concluding that only with deep reluctance would the man part with Deliramma, said, "As her foster father, it would be your privilege to see her again whenever you returned this way."

At this, the merchant said, "Your Imperial Majesty, that would be a consolation. It is not easy to part with one who, like a true daughter, has long been dear to me. Moved, however, by thinking of her future and Your Majesty's generous thought for me, I accept your offer."

Thus he bowed to the emperor's wish.

In the days that followed, Deliramma, although unused to life in a palace, soon gained many of the courtly skills. Being young and strong, she learned how to ride a horse. Besides this, she quickly became accustomed to the wearing of jewels and handsome clothes.

In her speech, however, the fair young lady seemed a little strange in her new surroundings. Long used to the joking and easy talk of a caravan company, her words were sometimes rather free.

One day, when she was chatting with other ladies of

the court, the Princess Purandocht joined the gathering.

"See the necklace of white jade which His Imperial Majesty bought from the merchant for me," she said, holding up her shapely chin so that the gift could be admired.

"How like the early blossoms of a pear tree," said one of the ladies.

"As delicate as a spider's thread in the moonlight," said another.

"Like the sweet notes of songs Your Imperial Highness sings," said a third.

In a similar vein each of the ladies spoke with high praise of the emperor's gift, until at last it was the turn of Deliramma.

Many were the treasures she had seen in the merchant's caravan. So she said simply, "It becomes Your Highness well, but I have often seen much finer."

A sudden hush fell on the circle of ladies. Astonished by her words, they all sensed a pounding in their hearts; but they heard only the hum of a bee, which had flown into the room from the courtyard garden.

As for the princess, although at first she looked dazed with surprise, she soon showed that she had a merry heart. She laughed and said, "Well, now I know what you think."

Thus the moment passed; but when she had left the company, the other ladies crowded about Deliramma.

"How could you speak so to the princess?" said one.

"In a palace, one's tongue must ever be under heavy guard," said another.

"Each word spoken before our ruling family should be clothed in silk to rustle on its way," counselled a third.

Not a little distressed, Deliramma resolved to be more cautious, but she remained in constant danger of making sad mistakes.

Now as time went by, it happened that very often the emperor asked Deliramma for a song. When she sang, he listened with rapt delight. Indeed, he was so charmed by her voice as well as her beauty that he said to her many tender things.

Happy in her company, Vahram came to find that he could ill bear any day in which he failed to see her, and even went so far as to invite her to accompany him on a hunt. When she accepted with a smile of delight, he instantly gave commands for all to be arranged.

On the appointed day, a large number of imperial retainers were awake and up long before the dawn. Mounted upon elephants, they rode through the forests, gradually driving a great many lions, wild asses, boars, and deer into a vast enclosed park. It was in the woods and marshland here that the emperor liked to hunt.

When all was in readiness, Vahram, Deliramma, and a notable company of courtiers set out on horses. The imperial party was preceded by twenty-one musicians who, taking their places in a stand prepared for them in the park, could be heard playing lively and encouraging music when the emperor and his guests arrived.

Very soon, Vahram spotted a handsome stag some

distance off beyond a marshy river. It pleased his fancy to pursue this particular deer, so he ordered two barges, one of medium size for Deliramma, and a large one for himself.

After they and the oarsmen were aboard, a harpist entered each of the boats. They would play for the passengers until such time as the emperor might order all music to be hushed lest it frighten away the quarry.

While the two boats glided near each other across the river, and merry tunes were sounding in the air, Deliramma said to the emperor, "Pray, Sir, let me see if with a single arrow you are able to hit yonder stag on one ear and on one hindfoot, both at the same time."

For a moment the emperor looked puzzled. Then asking that the music be stilled, he stood up where he was in the imperial barge and took in his hands the bow which had been slung about his neck. After drawing an arrow from a quiver held by one of his men, he took aim with precise care before he shot.

Flying very straight, the arrow touched some fur on the tip of the deer's left ear. Immediately, the stag, as he might have done if tickled by a branch or annoyed by a bee, raised his left hindfoot and brushed his ear with it.

Seizing this instant, the emperor shot a second arrow. Neatly, it glanced off the creature's lifted hoof and grazed his ear at the same time.

While the startled animal ran away, the courtiers, observing Vahram's feat, not only cheered him but also put out in small boats to join their ruler.

"The skill of Your Majesty," said one, "is as marvelous as music."

"Your Majesty's arrow," said another, "flew to its mark as surely as a bird to its nest."

"Never before," said a third, "have we seen a strategem so clever."

Soon around the emperor there was a great hubbub of congratulations as all the boats bearing his courtiers drew near the imperial barge.

Highly pleased with himself, Vahram turned to Deliramma.

"Well, well, my Dear," he said, "I have listened long enough to these others. Pray, what have *you* to say?"

Now the young lady had found the emperor's feat amusing as well as clever. So she laughed lightly, and then without thinking, began to joke.

"Really now," she said, "there was nothing so remarkable in what you did. Anyone could have done as well had he only known the trick."

A clap of silence fell upon the company. No one spoke. The courtiers heard only the sound of a little water dripping from a raised oar, and the quack of a wild duck flying high above them.

Vahram was shocked and wounded. Especially so because Deliramma's laughter and strange words had been uttered in front of many of his courtiers.

Hot anger rose within him, and, overpowered by rage, words caught in his throat.

Finally, even though deep within him he loved Deliramma, his fury swelled to such a peak that he gasped, "Take her away; take her far away. Remove her silken cloak and precious jewels. Let her be driven into the darkest forest and there be devoured by beasts."

Then he had himself rowed back to the land, mounted his horse, and sped at a gallop along the mountain road to his palace. As he did so, a storm broke over his head, but he scarcely noticed the lightning, which zigzagged across the sky, nor the soaking rain which followed.

As for Deliramma, the guards removed her cloak and jewels. These sparkled fitfully as sudden streaks of light brightened the stormy sky. Making her leave the boat in which she had been seated, the men drove her through the watery marshland, out of the hunting park, and alone and unarmed into the darkest part of the forest. There they left her while a heavy rain beat down about her head.

In the palace of the emperor, it was very quiet. Vahram shut himself up in his own apartments, and everyone walked softly.

Someone whispered, "She is an ungrateful girl, for the emperor loved her. Besides, no one must be allowed to laugh at our ruler."

Another said simply, "Our emperor must be very sad, because Deliramma is beautiful, and because he loved her."

And Vahram, once his first fierce anger had abated, became suddenly uneasy. He thought a moment, and then as quickly as before, he acted.

Flinging open his doors, he gave commands in a voice as sharp as lightning, as urgent as thunder. To the guards of the palace and to those who had driven Deliramma away, he gave new instructions.

"Hurry to the north and south. Hurry to the east and west. If need be, turn my entire empire upside down, but find fair Deliramma. Even at this moment a lion may be at her throat. I cannot bear to have her suffer. I cannot bear to have her gone."

So the guards rode off in search. And the anxious emperor walked back and forth, back and forth, as he waited for news of his missing love.

When it came time to eat, Vahram's face was long and sorrowful. The imperial cooks had prepared all of his favorite foods; but he tasted only a little rose petal pilau and called for some pussywillow broth.

Every few moments he stood up and looked out to see if anyone was coming back with Deliramma, but none of the guards could find her. The search continued for many days. Crashing through the forests on elephants and racing along the imperial roads on horses, the men pursued every rumor of where she might be.

Unfortunately, the rain had washed away her footprints, and each disappointment was followed by another. At last, grieving deeply, the emperor gave up hope and became ill with unhappiness. He stopped going out of doors; and because Deliramma was not there to sing, he would allow no music within his palace.

Although many noted doctors came to see him and consulted daily with each other, none of their herbs and other medicines seemed to improve his pitiful condition. Finally, he decided to put all these aside and await the return and advice of his three young friends who had gone to recover the Mirror of Justice.

The sister of the emperor was usually as cheerful as the sound of a brook of cool water. But now the hours for her were not only lonely with Vijayo away, but empty of pleasure with her brother so ill. To pass the time as she also waited for the return of the three young men, she composed this sad song, which she dared to recite only in whispers:

PANTOUM FOR AN EMPEROR

The heart of every hour dies
As swiftly as young lions bound,
And while our Emperor Vahram sighs
Till Deliramma can be found.

As swiftly a young lions bound,
His palace guards pursue the quest
Till Deliramma can be found
Between the endless East and West.

His palace guards pursue the quest,
And while our Emperor Vahram sighs,
Between the endless East and West
The heart of every hour dies.

THE

Dangerous Demon

The three princes crossed the desert by camel. Then, once more on horseback, they found themselves with many travelers in India.

Their road lay between luxuriant forests, where bulbuls sang in the daylight, and tigers prowled at night. Around the villages the country people had built high walls, so they slept when it was dark and awoke smiling with the sun.

Late one afternoon, the three brothers came to the country of the Vakatakas and in it to a village with a few houses of mud bricks and thatched roofs. Here also was a large farm for the raising of peacocks. These stately birds had black eyes, feathery crowns, and turquoise tails, bright with circles of blue, which looked like strangely glowing eyes.

Learning they had visitors, the people ran out of their homes and welcomed the three young men. The people bowed, pressed their hands together in greeting, and led the brothers into the cool shade of an old asoka tree. Its blossoms, the colors of a thousand tiny fires, were reflected gold and red in a curving pool.

Among the villagers was their headman. Bowing politely, he asked the brothers if he might render them any service.

"I thank you for your kindness," Balakrama said. "We are traveling to the country of Queen Parvathi, hoping to execute an errand for His Imperial Majesty, the Emperor Vahram of Persia."

An expression of both astonishment and awe crossed the face of the headman.

He said, "Our village is honored by your presence, for I perceive that you have entered into the councils of the great. Permit me to conduct you to a nearby monastery. In that place you will be suitably received and may talk with men of learning like yourselves."

Great was the surprise of the three princes when they were led to a monastery lodged in the steep face of a rocky hillside. Even more were they amazed when, drawing nearer, they discovered that here, made all of stone, were porches, columns, and carvings as intricate as if they had been formed of wood. Moreover it was clear from the sound of metal striking upon stone that the cutting of rock was still going forward.

At this strange and vast establishment, the princes were welcomed by a chief monk, the abbot in charge, and invited to stay as long as they could. He gave them a place to rest and a supper of millet, fresh butter, and beans.

The next day, he showed them many monks in yellow robes, hard at work, carving room after room out of the solid rock. Some were living quarters with tables and couches of stone. One was a chapel with a wondrously sculptured figure of Buddha. Also there were several halls, immense in size. These had been plastered, then ornamented with pictures of men and women, saints and kings, and scenes of horses, elephants, geese, and flowering lotus plants. The artist monks had painted them with such sure strokes, in black, red, yellow, green and creamy white, that they seemed to have been done by magic.

As soon as possible the three brothers talked to the abbot about their earnest hope of overcoming the Fearsome Hand.

"If the tree of success should bow in our favor," Balakrama said, "we shall beg Her Majesty, Queen Parvathi, to let us pluck the Mirror of Justice as one would pluck a ripe mango and take it back to Persia."

"Then you will be welcome, indeed," the abbot said. "The magic glass now spares her country something of grief, for the Hand no longer moves to seize upon men and cast them into the sea; however, the mirror does not prevent the dreadful apparition of the Hand itself nor the terror it inspires."

"I pray we may be fortunate," Vijayo said, "in helping to remove this terrible affliction."

"I have no doubt," the abbot said, "that you will try your utmost. Therefore I shall send news of your arrival to the governor of our district that he may aid you on your way. Allow me to warn you, however, that many have tried and many have failed at what you propose to do. All were turned back by a mighty demon named Asura, who delights in the terror which the Hand inspires."

"And how did he thwart them?" said Rajahsingha.

In reply, the abbot explained, "To reach the country of Queen Parvathi, and even the city of our own governor, one must cross a river. Beyond it lies the forest stronghold of Asura. Although he dwells inside the earth, his seven arms are all of such great strength that he can raise the very earth beneath a horse and unseat any rider whom he chooses.

"Many young men have been thrown headlong to the ground. Others he has driven back, mounted still but faint with fear. For these have seen the road become so steep along its course and so full of danger with falling trees and rolling boulders that they could not stay upon it."

"This is news of vast import," Vijayo said, "but tell me, pray, how can Asura know of our intent to overcome the Fearsome Hand?"

"It has been said from ancient times," the kindly abbot answered, "that through the cracks and fissures of the earth, he can look upon a man's eyes and read therein the purpose of his heart and mind. For the sake of your lives, therefore, it might be best not to pursue further the object you have stated."

The princes bowed and thanked the abbot for his warning. But being full of courage, they were not dissuaded from their purpose.

When he saw that their minds remained unchanged, the abbot said, "I shall search our ancient books. Perhaps in these, some way may be described to circumvent Asura."

The three brothers thanked him and slept peacefully through the night. When they awoke, he was looking down upon them with grave and tired eyes.

"I have perused our books of sacred meaning and of magic lore," he told them, a sadness in his voice, "but nothing certain have I found on overcoming demons. Only one passage may be helpful in this matter."

He unrolled a small scroll, made from strips of palm leaves, and read:

" 'One feather from a peacock's tail
In wisdom's hand may oft prevail.' "

Vijayo said, "Pray tell us how we should construe this."

"Alas," the abbot said, "I cannot do so. Still, it is possible to follow even a dark saying part of the way. Therefore, with my prayers, I present to each of you one feather from a peacock's tail. May they serve you well."

The princes accepted these gifts with many thanks, though wondering how they might be employed.

The way to the district capital was long, and while the brothers waited for word from the governor, they

wandered freely about the monastery looking at its great pictures. One day they stopped beside a young artist monk who had just finished the portrait of an old man.

His painting was very softly bathed in sunshine, reflected from the sky by a mirror of polished metal. This had been set in an outer doorway to cast light inside upon the wall.

The princes stood beside the young artist and admired his work. With great skill he had used reddish brown for the wrinkled skin and black lines for the old man's short beard and sparse hair. But the eyes had been painted in white, as bright and shining as the garment falling around his lean body.

"Now there was a wide-awake fellow," Balakrama said, "and you have drawn him with much spirit."

"A strange man," the artist said. "He came to us on foot, a tired traveler. After I had given him something to eat, I persuaded him, but only with some difficulty, to sit here a few moments that I might study him for this painting.

"At first, as you said, he seemed wide-awake, but I believe he was very weary; for in as short a time as it takes a young lion to jump across a brook, he fell asleep. Then an odd thing happened."

"Pray, what?" said Rajahsingha.

"Without his waking," the young monk replied, "this old fellow's lips began to move, forming softly spoken words, all clothed in verse."

The princes looked at one another.

"And what did he say?" asked Balakrama.

"Now that would be hard to tell," the artist answered, "for his speech was not only swift but somewhat mumbled. Moreover, when suddenly the sound of stonecutting rose with special loudness, he awoke trembling and was silent."

"I beg you, stir your memory," Balakrama said. "Can you recall any fragment of the verse?"

The young man looked thoughtful for a moment.

"Only this," he said. Then slowly, as if searching in a dark woodland of his mind, he recited just these two lines:

> "One may seek but cannot borrow
> This mystery lying close to sorrow."

"How like the others!" Vijayo whispered to his brothers.

"Here, look here," Balakrama said. He pointed to something in the picture they had not noticed earlier. "What held he here?"

"A case made of silver, I believe," the artist said. "Perhaps for scrolls of writing. He had it hidden under his cloak. Only when that slipped aside as he nodded, did I see it."

Rajahsingha said, "As surely as this floor of rock is firm beneath us, he was Aphoenicius."

At this moment, the abbot came into the hall bearing a message from the governor of the district. He would deem it an honor to receive the three young men as visitors, and had sent an officer to be their guide. The brothers, therefore, soon made ready to depart.

Before leaving the hall, however, Rajahsingha said to the artist, "Pray, tell us, when last did you see this old one whom your talent has so brilliantly depicted?"

"Your words robe me in undue honor," the young monk said, modestly, "but I can tell you he was here this morning, and when leaving, started towards our district capital."

"Thither do we go," Rajahsingha said. "And with our horses we can surely overtake a traveler on foot."

In haste, therefore, the three brothers thanked the abbot, the artist, and others at the monastery. And after the two lines of verse had been written down on some long strips of talipot palm leaves, they set out swiftly with their guide.

Hoping to find the ancient seer with his formula, the three brothers rode so fast that the ground itself seemed hurrying to meet them. But though they saw men working in fields, women carrying jars of water on their heads, and hundreds of people traveling, nowhere did they glimpse even the shadow of an old man with flashing eyes and a cylinder of silver.

At last, they neared a wide river where a small ferry took men and beasts, two at a time, across the water.

Here their guide said, "Before we venture on that ferry, tell me if by any chance you come with purpose to subdue the Fearsome Hand."

"That is our hope," said Balakrama.

The governor's officer reined in his horse, and his face became long and gloomy.

"Stop now," he said. "Turn back; for as soon as you have crossed this river, even before you try to follow the road which you see going through the forest, a demon named Asura will in your eyes perceive the purpose of your hearts.

"And what will befall then?" Rajahsingha asked.

"Once across the river," the officer said, "You will have to flee from falling trees and thundering boulders. The land itself will rise and shake beneath you. I beg you, Worthy Gentlemen, go no farther."

Rajahsingha paused and then said to his brothers, "Who knows? Perhaps Asura will be away or even fail to guess our errand. I pray you, wait here with our guide, for I am strongly minded to test this matter for myself."

His brothers tried to prevent him, each saying he would be the first to cross the river. But since only one man and his horse could go at a time, and Rajahsingha had spoken bravely, it was finally agreed that he should have his way.

As the ferryman rowed him across the river, the youngest prince said to him, "Tell me, have you taken in your boat today an old man with eyes that flash like fire—an old man carrying a cylinder of silver?"

"It is strange that you should ask this," the man replied, "for on the shore behind us this very morning there was an old fellow matching your description. I hurried to take him in my boat, but when I reached the bank and looked up, I saw only a great bird flying. He had fiery eyes and shining feathers like the golden one of Indra."

"Did anyone else see it also?" said Rajahsingha.

"None that I know," replied the man. "I have asked

many whom I ferried here today, but each, it seems, was too busy thinking of what he had left behind or of what he would find ahead, to glance up at the sky."

The boat soon reached the bank of the river near the forest of Asura. Rajahsingha thinking only of the boatman's story and not of coming danger, paid his fare and, leading his horse, stepped slowly off onto the shore.

At once his thoughts were changed. His feet had barely reached the ground when a deep fissure opened before him in the earth, and there was a great roar like a thousand lions. The ground beneath him trembled, and the land which lay ahead began to rise up and up until it was as high as a mountain. The road, which had stretched smooth and level, ran almost straight uphill. At a distance it was lost to sight in a bank of lowering clouds. Rajahsingha stood aghast.

"Come back! Come back!" the ferryman shouted above the terrific din. "A mighty demon lives beneath this land. Surely your eyes betrayed some goal that has enraged him. Come, sir. Come. Let me take you back at once!"

Rajahsingha hesitated for a moment. Then when he saw giant trees falling over and tremendous boulders tumbling against each other and rolling down the side of the mountain, he ran back with his frightened horse onto the boat.

As soon as the ferry set out upon the river, the strange elevation slowly began to sink. With much rumbling and hissing, it once more became level land. The noise, too, finally subsided.

When the youngest prince had joined his brothers, he found them nearly overwhelmed with astonishment. Yet all three were still undaunted in their purpose. The guide, however, looked very solemn.

"Now that you have seen what the demon can do," he said, "I beg you not to anger him again by pressing forward."

"But is there no remedy?" Vijayo said.

"None that I know of," the governor's officer said, "so long as Asura can read the purpose in one's eyes. And who can change his face?"

"Who, indeed?" Balakrama said.

His glance had fallen upon the peacock feather given him by the abbot. On it, shaped like eyes, were small blue circles.

The oldest prince held a feather in front of his face so that the upper part of his visage appeared turquoise in color, with two new and strangely glowing eyes of blue. The feather covered his eyes, yet he could see his way through the tiny openings between its particles.

"Let me make trial," Balakrama said, "of this small device which hides my eyes."

So the ferryman, with some reluctance, took the oldest prince and his horse across the river. Once there, Balakrama stepped ashore. Holding the horse's reins in his left hand, he kept his eyes hidden with the peacock feather, held in his right hand. Like Rajahsingha, he saw a fissure in the earth, but the ground beyond seemed firm and still. He advanced a step. No boulders fell, no trees were toppled. He moved again, and still no disturbance seemed to come. At last he ran forward; and even then the land stood firm beneath him. There was now no question. Asura had been outwitted.

When his two brothers saw that all was well, they were full of joy and hastened to cross the river. Each covered his eyes with a peacock feather. The guide came also but without concern; for his country's visitors seemed well protected, and he himself had made no resolve to oppose the Fearsome Hand.

After all the travelers had been rowed across the river, they thanked and paid the ferryman, then hastily set out over the land where deep below Asura lived. Masking their eyes, the three princes rode along without mishap, and soon the demon's woods were well behind them.

Not until then did they pause, and not until then did Rajahsingha tell his brothers what the ferryman had earlier told him about the old man and the golden bird.

"So strong is the magic of Aphoenicius," Balakrama said, "I doubt not that he can as easily take the form of a bird as of a man. So I believe the ferryman spoke truly, and once more we have missed the aged seer."

"This I think, too," Vijayo said, with a sigh as sad as the sound of autumn wind sweeping through a bamboo grove.

So the three brothers were once more discouraged in their search for the formula. Having at last reached the city of the district governor, however, they were met and greeted with honor and rejoicing, which much raised their spirits.

"Thrice three times you are welcome to our country, this city, and my house," the governor said. "Not only do I hear that you are come to oppose the Fearsome Hand, but also that the mighty demon, Asura, was no match for your courage and your cunning. Hence shall we endeavor to show you the tree of our welcome and the fruit of our gratitude."

At these words, the three princes bowed, and Balakrama said, "Thank you for your courteous welcome; but not yet have we succeeded in our purpose towards the Hand, and it was one of your own countrymen who gave us the means to thwart Asura's power."

Delighted by the modesty of his visitors, the governor called in the members of his council. The first to come was a leader of caravans. He wished to provide the princes with a large company of men and camels for their journey to the country of Queen Parvathi. The second was a *shresthin*, a banker, who offered to send letters to his many friends, so that the three might be welcomed and rest their heads in comfort along the way.

A goldsmith was the third. He gave each of the princes a chain of finest gold and to them all a letter to the leader of his guild in Her Majesty's capital.

Finally there came a scribe, who wrote on palm leaves with a piece of iron. Soon he had sent off all of the letters, including one from the governor to Queen Parvathi. This went by special courier to let her know as soon as possible that important visitors were on their way.

Accepting with many thanks all of these kind and unexpected offers, the three brothers went to stay in the residence of the governor until all had been prepared for their further journey. Then, taking leave with added thanks, they set out once more.

Like his brothers, Prince Vijayo was deeply moved by all the kindness he had met, but he often sighed as he thought of the fair Princess Purandocht whom he had left in Persia. He knew that with the distance of each day's journey she was farther away. Nevertheless, the memory of her joyous singing gave him a lighter heart. So, thinking of her, he made this song:

PANTOUM FOR THE PRINCESS PURANDOCHT

My heart will always hear your song;
Asura cannot hide the sound
Though the earth may rumble long
With his anger underground.

Asura cannot hide the sound
While woodlands slide and boulders roll
With his anger underground
When he learns our princely goal.

While woodlands slide and boulders roll
Though the earth may rumble long
When he learns our princely goal,
My heart will always hear your song.

THE

Fearsome Hand

Before the three princes had reached the royal capital, the queen sent a party of counselors to welcome them to her country. Among these was the *mahamantrin,* her prime minister. He addressed the princes and politely inquired the purpose of their visit.

"We have come for our friend, the Emperor Vahram," Balakrama said, "that we may attempt to deliver your noble queen and her fair country from the scourge of the Fearsome Hand. Also, if fortune gives us success, we shall humbly beg Her Majesty to let us bring back to Persia the Mirror of Justice."

When the mahamantrin fully understood what the

young men wished, he immediately sent word to Queen Parvathi. Without delay, the brothers were invited to visit the royal palace and to enter the capital on three great elephants, which she sent to bring them.

These mountainous beasts had skins that were nearly white, long ears, and eyes of a delicate pink. Around their foreheads were golden circlets like narrow crowns from which hung ornaments and harnesses bedecked with gems.

The three brothers rode on high seats behind drivers dressed in white. Royal servants walked beside the elephants and with parasols on tall poles kept the princes shaded from the sun. As they proceeded in this way, the party's progress was trumpeted upon a conch shell by one of Her Majesty's musicians, who marched ahead.

At the sound he made, throngs came out to see the honored visitors. The women were dressed in their finest clothes and adorned with earrings, beads, and anklets. Men and children ran alongside the guests and tried to get more than a passing glimpse of the three strangers.

When at last the brothers arrived at the capital, they were led through streets where small shops sold tempting sweets, red and white lotus flowers, and fragrant perfumes to passersby. Tall mansions rose in many places, and other wonders on all sides seized their eyes until at last, they reached the palace.

It stood near the center of the city surrounded by a high wall, in the midst of a park bright with the orange color of flowering kadamba trees. Seven stories high, the queen's residence was, built around a great courtyard garden.

Being royal guests, the three brothers were led to sumptuous apartments, and provided with many luxuries for their comfort and delight. Beside each canopied bed, were palm-leaf books and a drawing table with brushes and colors. A window on one side gave a splendid view of the courtyard, with yellow-flowered campaka trees around a small lake and fountain. Also in each room, a stringed lute hung on the wall; and nearby was placed a squared board for games.

After the princes had rested and put on the fine robes which Vahram had given them, they were greeted by a large company of nobles and led through four great halls, each larger than the one before. The first was ornamented by wide sheets of cast metal, skillfully incised with pictures and poems from ancient stories. The second had walls of wood, carved with hundreds of figures of men and elephants in a great procession. The third was brilliant with paintings, telling the history of the royal house and the brave exploits of its many monarchs.

Nevertheless, the fourth surpassed in beauty all the others, for its walls were decked with jewels, and in it the princes saw a royal throne set with shining rubies. These and the other precious gems, the courtiers said, were of an uncommon and magic sort, so brilliant that even on the darkest nights they illumined the whole room.

In this place of glittering splendor, the queen received the princes. And to them, she matched the room in which she sat. Her alabaster complexion was framed by dark hair drawn to a soft knot at the back of her graceful neck, and on her head rested a delicate golden crown set with hundreds of diamonds.

Her jacket was of satin, softly green. Against it glistened an emerald necklace. Her long skirt, dancing with shimmering lights, was of the finest Indian silk and woven in many bands, some golden like the sun and others white like blossoms of the jasmine vine.

Much affected by her elegance, the three princes bowed very low. Then they presented her with gifts from the emperor. These were great quantities of silk brocade, a golden necklace set with peridots, and several books written in an exquisite hand, containing the most engaging stories Vahram knew.

The queen conversed with her visitors and thanked them.

She said, "Our hearts welcome you, and I perceive that in your persons kindness and courage meet with mighty rivers of strength and wisdom."

After listening and speaking to them longer, she promised to return to Persia the Mirror of Justice, providing the three young men could in some manner bring to an end the threat of the Fearsome Hand.

When their audience was over, the princes were invited into still another great room. This one had walls of sandalwood and tables made of porphyry and jasper. Here, while musicians delighted their ears with cheerful tunes, the brothers were entertained at a banquet by a number of the greatest men of the court. So lavish was the feast of curried rice flavored with tamarind, fresh lentils, tender cakes, and rich fruits of the mango and plantain trees, that it lasted long into the night.

Nevertheless, the three brothers were up the next morning before dawn, and with the queen, her officers, and other noblemen of the court, went down to the shore of the sea. Hardly had the sun risen when a terrifying sight came into view.

A gigantic right hand with its five fingers extended rose up from the water and soared high into the sky. The brothers not only stood amazed, but even their courage was overtaken by a chilling blast of fear.

For hours they watched the terrible thing. Until the sun was high, it moved slowly along the highroad of the sky or paused here and there, hovering in place. Then suddenly, at noon, it started upon a frightening descent, moving toward the very place where Queen Parvathi and the others stood.

When this happened, the courtiers were ready. The Mirror of Justice had been placed on the shore, close to the edge of the water.

"In past days, before we had the glass," the queen said, "the great Hand at any moment of the day might snatch a man from the shore, the city, or a farm and fling him into the sea. People were afraid to leave their homes, yet those whose work led out of doors had to take the horrible risk of being seized. Today you can see how the Mirror prevents such a dreadful raid."

The princes watched as the courtiers tilted the glass at an angle to reflect the Hand. As they did so, the strange phenomenon in the sky, without seizing any-one, began to sink back. Finally, slowly, it disappeared

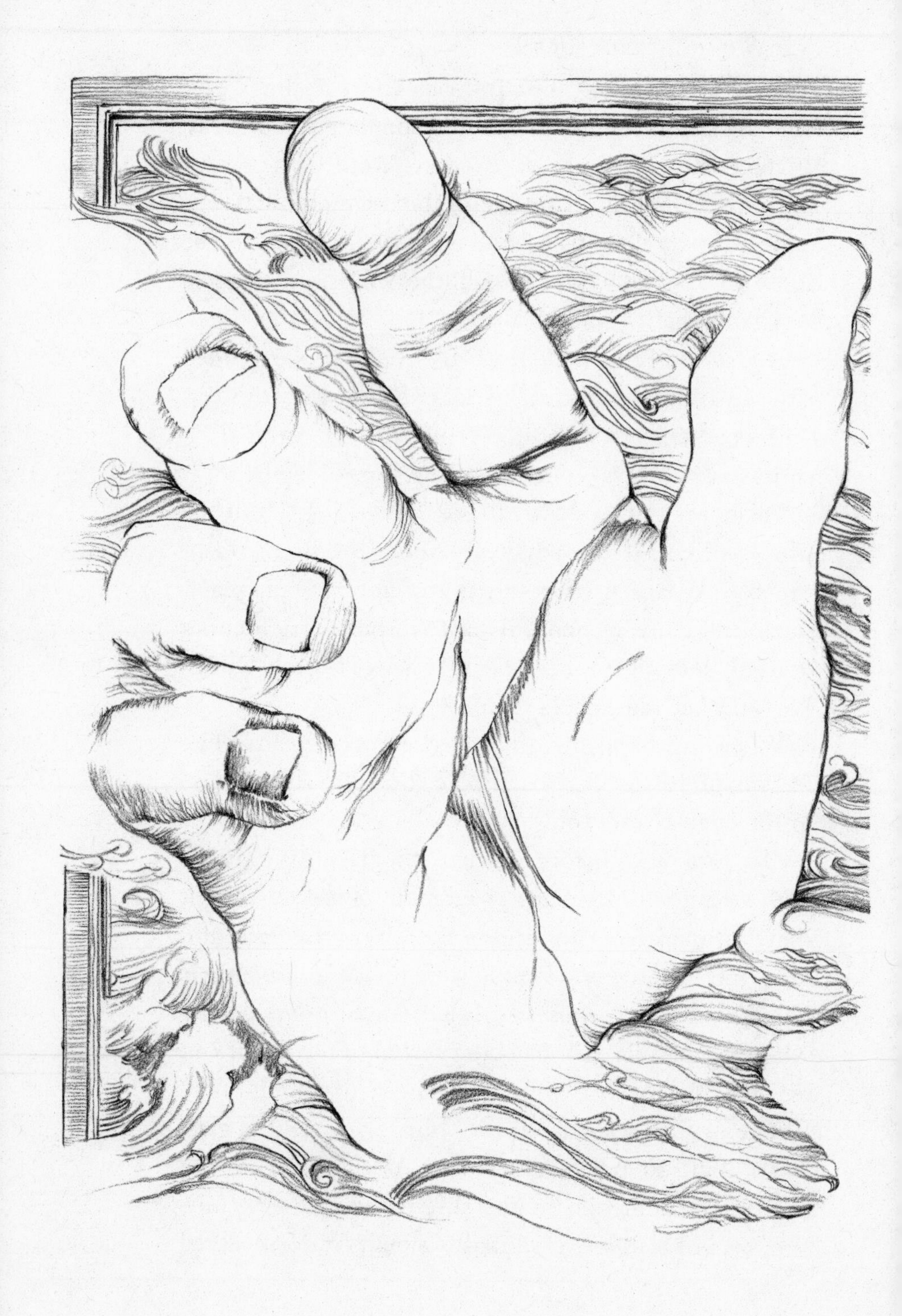

below the waves, from whence it had come.

That night the three brothers consulted among themselves.

"The Hand seems very bold," Balakrama said.

"Until it sees its own reflection," Vijayo said.

"If boldness drives boldness away," said Rajahsingha, "then what we need is courage. I pray you, let me face this thing alone to try its meaning. I believe I know its purpose; for much reading in the lore of justice, now leads me to believe it can be tamed.

With much reluctance, the others finally agreed, though this seemed a greater danger than any of them yet had faced. The next morning, the queen, her courtiers, and the two oldest princes of Serendip, stayed inside the palace. The Mirror of Justice and all the other people stayed indoors, too. Rajahsingha alone went down to the shore of the sea.

As soon as the sun came up, the terrible Hand moved slowly out of the water. With five fingers extended, it rose higher and higher. The queen and her people watched in silence from the windows of their homes, as the great Hand hovered high in the sky while the prince stood alone on the shore. The Hand was more quiet than it oftimes was, and the prince gazed up in silence. Then, just as the sun began to set, the Hand began a fierce descent. Rushing like a comet, it plummeted toward the very spot where Rajahsingha stood.

All the birds stopped twittering. Small animals scuttled away with fright. And as the young man watched the great Hand swooping towards him out of the deep blue heights of sky, he could not but wonder if his plan were right.

But though the terrible scourge, racing through the air, came nearer and nearer, the valor of the prince's heart held firm. He closed one eye against the sunlight and held out his bare right hand like a shield before his face. No sooner had he done so, than the Fearsome Hand seemed suddenly no larger than his own. At this Prince Rajahsingha laughed aloud.

Upon the instant, as if surprised by so much courage, the great Hand ceased advancing and hovered for a moment in one place. In this brief comma of time, the prince lifted up his hand again with all but two of his fingers folded. No sooner had he done so, than his adversary plunged straight down. It disappeared into the sea with a mighty splash; and Rajahsingha stood alone upon the sand.

When Queen Parvathi, who had watched the whole day through, saw this happen, she was filled with joy and wonder, and her people with her. The latter thought that the three visitors, and especially the youngest, must be more than mortal.

So great, so overwhelming was their relief, their gratitude, their joy, that they were eager to bow down and worship their deliverers. This, however, the three young princes would not permit.

The queen called all three to her, and the gratefulness of her heart was exceeded only by the curiosity of her mind. "By what strange skill and wisdom, has the Fearsome Hand now been subdued," she asked, once she had praised the deed that had been done.

Balakrama said, "Your Majesty, it was the valor of our youngest brother that overcame the Hand; for everywhere, as you must know, true courage meets with quick respect. Yet there was also more to this strange and fortunate event, which he can best explain.

"Pray do," she said, smiling and turning to Rajahsingha.

The third prince bowed and said, "Since Your Beauteous Majesty asks, I may say that the Hand was sent by a power that would try you, and had a particular message to deliver. By extending five fingers it endeavored to say that if only five persons in a great nation were well united, they could control the people. It was because the Hand had not been able to make this message clear and, in consequence, was full of fury, that it acted with so much violence."

"And why did you hold up your own hand with all but two fingers folded?" she asked.

"By doing so," Rajahsingha said, "I acknowledged the message and also signified that if only two persons were well united, they also could exercise control. I believe this, O, Great and Gentle Queen, for as you well know, two persons joined in a just cause will draw others unto them."

Queen Parvathi, marveled over and over at the wisdom of the three young strangers visiting her. Then she proclaimed a day of celebration in honor of the princes. At her word the mahamantrin assembled a great company of musicians, dancers, and actors to entertain and perform a play by a great poet whose name was Kalidasa.

It was to be given in a courtyard of the palace with a stage set at one end.

As soon as the queen with the nobles of her court and the three princes of Serendip had arrived and been seated, two of the performers came out, one in the role of a stage manager and the other as an actress. After low bows to the queen and her guests, the first player said they had come to give a play in honor of the three brave young visitors to their country.

Speaking to his companion, he said, "What then shall we present?"

The actress smiled and replied, "Let it be *Sakuntala.*"

So, while the three princes sat entranced, a play of great sadness, beauty, and joy unfolded before them. They saw Sakuntala, a beautiful lady, cast into sorrow. This was because her husband, King Dushyanta, bemused by a magic spell, could not recognize her as his own true bride. In the end, however, a wonderful ring restored his memory and happiness to them both.

When the play was over, Prince Rajahsingha saw tears still glistening in the eyes of young Queen Parvathi.

"We have seen a story," he said, "which moves in beauty like the clouds, sometimes dark with storms, sometimes bright with the dawn. I notice, however, that your eyes are still sad even though the tale ends happily for Sakuntala and for the king, her husband."

"Alas," the queen said, "never do I see this play, but I think of Princess Padmini, my own poor younger sister. Even now she may be wandering through the world, unrecognized by strangers or herself."

"How can this be?" Rajahsingha said.

"It is a sad history," the queen replied, "but since you ask, I will tell it to you. Many years ago, my grandfather dreamed of a strange white horse and also of a magician who said, 'Withersoever this noble animal goes in the space of a single year, the land shall be yours to own and the peoples yours to protect.'

"Soon after he saw a white charger standing in a bamboo grove near the gates of his palace. Believing this to be a clear sign of his duty, he called in a company of soldiers, and said, 'Follow yonder horse which now is pawing the ground beside my bamboo trees. Withersoever it wanders in the space of a full year, take the lands in my name and inform the peoples living on them of my full protection.'

"The soldiers obeyed, and everywhere the horse happened to stray, men and women welcomed the protection of the king, my grandfather—all, that is, except members of one fierce tribe. These drove the soldiers back and were long our enemies.

"It was one of their nation, we believe, who many years ago expressed his hatred of us by stealing away my sister, when both of us were tiny children. Perhaps he meant to hold her for ransom but changed his mind. Of this my father had no word, nor have we ever seen her again."

Hearing this story, the three brothers were greatly moved, especially Rajahsingha. Tears welled into his eyes and ran down his cheeks.

"Would that we could restore her to you," he said.

"Is there any way by which she might be known?"

"My father told me that on the day she disappeared, her dress was of palest blue silk, and she wore about her throat a necklace of tiny links in the shape of crowns. So long has she been gone from us, however, that by now these things could easily be lost."

The queen paused for a moment, then said, "Enough. It is not meet that I should burden you, who are our honored guests, with family sorrows."

Prince Rajahsingha said, "Like an autumn vine bowed with the glory of its clustered grapes, we are honored to bear even a tiny share of Your Majesty's royal grief." Then he breathed a sigh of deep sympathy and bowed before her.

Queen Parvathi was so touched by his kindness that once again she smiled. Then, musicians having appeared before them, the rest of the day was given over to concerts, feasting, and other happy pastimes.

Even so, the princes began to think of going back to Persia.

"Let us hope that the queen will be ready now to restore the Mirror of Justice to the Emperor Vahram," Balakrama said. "The sooner our errand is accomplished, the sooner we may hope to gain our father's permission to return to Serendip."

Vijayo said, "We must also continue our search for *Death to Dragons,* and for Aphoenicius. Then looking thoughtful for a long time, he made and sang this song:

PANTOUM FOR APHOENICIUS

Where the sudden mountains grow
This old one speeds on foot or wings.
He guards the word for dragon woe,
Long aeons sought by noble kings.

This old one speeds on foot or wings
With magic in a silver case,
Long aeons sought by noble kings,
A slippery shadow in the chase.

With magic in a silver case
He guards the word for dragon woe,
A slippery shadow in the chase
Where the sudden mountains grow.

THE

Queen's Question

Next day, Queen Parvathi summoned her counselors and asked them to gather in the jewelled hall of state. The first to come were the mahamantrin and the royal chaplin. Then arrived the treasurer, the minister of peace, and the keeper of the royal records. All of them bowed with deep respect when the queen, herself, entered the hall.

Noting quickly that all of her counselors were present, she spoke to them in this fashion: "My Princely Advisors, I seek your cherished opinion concerning the Mirror of Justice. As you know, it is much desired by our friend, the Emperor Vahram of Persia. Moreover, his three courageous emissaries have now subdued the Fearsome Hand. Should we not return the glass at once?"

The mahamantrin said, "Noble and Glorious Majesty, it is true that yesterday our three visitors, and particularly the youngest, did us a service of great valor. Never before have we seen the Fearsome Hand in such retreat. Besides, with this new day, it has not returned. Yet, how do we know it will not appear another time? Perhaps it will have another message we cannot discern. If that should happen, and we no longer had the Mirror of Justice, with what should we be protected?"

Queen Parvathi said, "I perceive that you have spoken after much pondering, O Great and Chief of my Royal Counselors. But I too have thought at length upon this matter, and now believe there is a way, without the glass, to be quite safe. Before I can reveal it, however, I must enjoin upon you the deepest secrecy."

The counselors bowed and said, "We shall be as silent as statues made of stone."

"For this I thank you," the queen said. "Now I shall tell you a thing which hitherto has long been hidden in my heart. Before the late king, my father, died, he said to me, 'My daughter, since one day you will inherit my vast dominions, many, in order to rule by your side, will seek your hand in marriage. I charge you, however, to take no one as a husband except a prince who can give the right reply to the question I now shall put before you.' He then explained what I should ask."

The counselors, who had not heard of this before,

listened with great attention.

"Judging by their courteous behavior," the queen said, "I believe our three young visitors to be of illustrious birth. I ask you to ascertain if this is so. If one of them is a prince and he can reply correctly to the question, I shall try to win him for my husband. With such a one at my side, surely the Fearsome Hand will never dare to come again."

The counselors applauded her words. "With two such united, as our youngest visitor proclaimed," one said, "no force could bring our nation grief." With this, the mahamantrin left to approach the three brothers.

"Towards you," he said, "we are full of gratitude for delivering our country from the dread power of the Fearsome Hand. Indeed, our noble queen has so much admiration for your valor and your kindness that she asks to know who you may be, and begs that this may no longer remain a secret from her."

The three princes, mindful of their duty to their father, had not told even the Emperor Vahram of their princely rank. Therefore they hesitated to reply.

"By your manner and appearance," the mahamantrin said, "no one will be persuaded that you are not at least of noble birth."

When the princes saw that their positions had been so nearly guessed, they answered, "We are three sons of Jaiya, the King of Serendip."

Hearing this, Queen Parvathi was filled with joy. She asked them all to appear before her.

"Your courage and sagacity in freeing my country

from the terror of the Fearsome Hand, emboldens me now to ask one more thing of you," she said. Here she hesitated a moment, then went on, "Before I do so, however, I beg you to consent to whatever I shall ask."

The princes, being very courteous and knowing that it is hard for ladies to be denied, agreed to do all that they could to fulfill her royal wish.

Whereupon, she posed her question, "Long ago, my father told me it was possible for one man in one day to eat a storage bin of salt, although he had never seen it tried. As you are men of genius, will you show me just how this may be done?"

Prince Rajahsingha said, "I believe, Your Royal Majesty, that the feat is not quite so difficult as some may have supposed. If I may be allowed until tomorrow for preparation, I offer to perform it in your royal presence."

Queen Parvathi was not a little surprised by the readiness of this response. But since her heart was already inclined towards the youngest prince, she was delighted that it was he who had made the offer. Very happily she gave him time in which to make ready and invited the brothers to appear before her again on the very next day.

When the three princes had returned to their apartments, Balakrama and Vijayo spoke to their youngest brother.

"I suppose," said the oldest prince, "that you have already made some plan."

"And what can we do to help you?" said the second prince.

Rajahsingha said, "First let us quickly find our letter to the chief goldsmith of this city, the one composed for us by the counselor of the governor. Now it will be useful."

The three brothers looked hurriedly through their belongings, and soon Balakrama found the letter.

Turning to Vijayo, Rajahsingha said, "In art you are the most accomplished. Pray sit here." He motioned to a chair near the drawing board. "And make a design such as I shall describe."

When Vijayo had drawn his plan, the three brothers set out with it to see the chief of goldsmiths. His shop stood on a broad street. Inside, it was dazzling with lights reflected from shining bowls, exquisite cups, and trays of gold.

From a back room where his helpers and workshop were, the master craftsman came out to receive his visitors. Even before he had read their letter, he said he would do all in his power to help them.

"Hither," said Rajahsingha, "we have brought a design of something needful to us." He showed the goldsmith Vijayo's drawing and continued, "Knowing that you excel in art and workmanship, we have come to ask if before the dawn tomorrow you can fashion out of gold what here you see designed."

When the great craftsman had studied Vijayo's drawing with care, he said, "Though it take the whole night through for all my men and me to complete this work, we shall still consider ourselves honored to serve you in this manner; for you have delivered our queen from the scourge of the Fearsome Hand."

Then he bowed very low.

When the following day came, the young Queen Parvathi decided to receive the three princes in a secluded part of her garden. Here peacocks stepped proudly across the grass, and ruddy sheldrakes floated upon the surface of a lotus pool.

On a hill nearby was a swing with long cords. Seated in it, Parvathi often delighted in soaring high above her China rose trees and even higher than the roof of her hall of state.

This day, however, she sat with dignity and grace on a bench of polished marble. There the young queen looked as fair as the white jasmine flowers in her dark hair, and her eyes were as bright as the golden threads woven into the silk of her light yellow robe.

"Your Royal Highnesses are very welcome in this garden," she said when the princes appeared before her. "May the shade of its trees keep you in comfort and the color of its flowers remind you ever of our warm friendship."

Then she addressed the youngest prince. "And now pray, show me," she said to Rajahsingha, "how a man may in one day eat the contents of an entire storage bin of salt."

Prince Rajahsingha bowed politely and said, "This, O Royal and Beauteous Majesty, I shall now endeavor to do."

Then he drew from under his cloak a tiny golden box. Skillfully wrought by the goldsmith following Vijayo's drawing, it was a storage bin in form and shape, but it was not much larger than a single pea.

The youngest prince opened the tiny box, and the queen could see that it was full of salt.

"Now I shall eat all the contents of this storage bin," said the prince, and he proceeded to do so easily and at once.

Queen Parvathi was charmed and delighted; but she said, "It is true that you have eaten all of the salt in that very small bin. Pray, tell me, though, what would you do with a very large bin where a great quantity of salt might be in store?"

Prince Rajahsingha bowed again and said, "Your Majesty, whoever eats a pinch of salt with a friend and does not know his duty toward him, will never know it even though he eat all of the salt in all of the storage bins of the world. As for me, I have tasted enough here to know I shall always have for you the deepest sentiments of respect and love."

The queen was enchanted. Not only had he solved the puzzle and given the reply her father had said would be the right one for her future husband, but his words had touched her heart.

Therefore she called her counselors to another meeting and revealed to them that the late king had told her to marry no one but a prince who would act and speak as the youngest visitor from Serendip had done.

"For this reason," she said, "and also because his courage and his wisdom have protected our country and won my heart, I urge you to speak to Prince Rajahsingha. Say that I offer him my hand, my heart, and the kingship of this country."

Thus commanded, the mahamantrin went at once to the youngest prince and said, "Our Queen has expressed great admiration for your merit and ability. Also, because of advice laid down by her father, the late king, and the promptings of her heart, she offers you her hand in marriage."

At these words, Prince Rajahsingha and both of his brothers were filled with surprise and delight. They decided that the high honor should be accepted if their father, the King of Serendip, approved.

Queen Parvathi hearing this, rejoiced also, and called the three princes, once again, before her. When they arrived, she told them that she would give the Mirror of Justice into their keeping to take back to the Emperor Vahram.

Then after she and the youngest prince had privately assured each other of their love and devotion, the three princes prepared to depart. The very next day they went to take their leave of Queen Parvathi. Repeatedly, she thanked them for all that they had done, and pressed upon them many gifts for the Emperor Vahram, for their father, and for themselves.

The youngest received a likeness of the queen. It was carved into one side of an oriental agate and set in a frame of diamonds. Moreover, Her Majesty also gave Rajahsingha a stringed lute, for she had heard that, like his brothers, he was deeply moved by music.

"Sweet melodies," she said, "have power to stir the memory. When these strings are touched to life, perchance your thoughts will turn to me."

"While absent from you, that will be my chiefest

pleasure and my comfort," said the youngest prince.

So the three brothers, not a little satisfied by their success in opposing the Fearsome Hand and by the happy offer of a royal marriage, started forth on the return trip to Persia. Before they had gone very far, however, a messenger from Serendip with an exceedingly grave expression upon his face met them on the road. He carried a letter from King Jaiya.

"What word have you of our father and our island?" Balakrama asked.

Their countryman dismounted from his horse, bowed, and said, "The news I must tell is dark with misfortune. His Majesty, our king, remains very ill, and not only are the great tanks of Serendip neglected, but the canals between them are clogged and sluggish, so that little water reaches the farms. Moreover, for a long time, no rain has fallen."

"Then surely our father calls us back to serve him and our people," Rajahsingha said, unsealing the letter. This, however, is what he read:

Vijayo was prudent to warn a mighty emperor of a plot against his life, but that is no more than any man would do for a friend. The dragons in the sea around our shores can never be dispersed with arrows, nor will just four lines of the magic formula enable us to prevail against them. So I perceive that my sons are still not ready to be called home or to serve as rulers.

At these words, the three brothers felt bowed and crushed. Consulting among themselves, they decided that this time Rajahsingha should compose the letter. This he did, sending word of their sorrow concerning the king's illness and earnestly requesting permission for his sons to return and help him in the matter of the great canals.

The letter also told the story of the conquest of the Fearsome Hand, enclosed the two lines of verse the old traveler had mumbled in the monastery, and said, *It seems that Aphoenicius can go not only in the guise of men but of a flying bird. How then can we ever hope to find him and obtain the whole formula? Pray, let us return and if need be, wrestle against the fierce dragons with our bare hands.*

Finally, Rajahsingha told King Jaiya of how the great and beautiful Queen Parvathi had offered him her heart and hand in marriage.

"Surely when he reads all of this," Rajahsingha said to his brothers, "he will be filled with joy and once more permit us to see his face in Serendip."

Heartened by this hope, the three brothers proceeded on their journey to Persia taking the Mirror of Justice with them. When occasionally they stopped to rest, Rajahsingha would often touch his lute with melodies agreeable to the heart. Then thinking of the one who had given him the instrument, he made and sang this song:

PANTOUM FOR QUEEN PARVATHI

Swing, Fair Star, above the pool
Higher than a hall of state.
Celestials bless your gentle rule
While I ride, and you must wait.

Higher than a hall of state
The Fearsome Hand no longer soars;
While I ride and you must wait
Till my return from other shores.

The Fearsome Hand no longer soars.
Celestials bless your gentle rule.
Till my return from other shores,
Swing, Fair Star, above the pool.

THE *Emperor's Malady*

The princes of Serendip journeyed happy in the knowledge that they had recovered the Mirror of Justice; but once more in Persia, other travelers met them with distressing news about the Emperor Vahram.

One said, "Our ruler must be very ill, because for a long time there have been no great feasts in the palace."

A second said, "His Imperial Majesty must indeed be sorely afflicted, for they say he allows no music in his hearing."

A third said, "Surely he must be suffering grievously for no longer does he appear before his people to hear in person that justice is done."

Much disturbed by these reports, the three princes nevertheless had to travel slowly on camels as they recrossed the desert. Then, mounted once more upon horses, the brothers rode swiftly again until they reached the village called Kuhabad.

Since their horses were too tired to go farther that day, the three brothers, although anxious to see the Emperor, decided to rest overnight in the village. Because they had paused here twice before in their travels, they were remembered by the people. The people had also heard by word of mouth of the conquest of the Hand and of how the Mirror of Justice was being returned.

Hence the princes were welcomed by all the people. The *dihqan,* who was the headman of the village, invited them to stay at his house. Here they were given a supper of eggplant, sweet rice, and purple grapes, while their host invited all the principal men of the place to come and visit.

At first the men asked the three brothers about their adventures in India, to which the brothers replied both briefly and modestly. Then the faces of the elders became dark with anxiety as they spoke of the emperor's illness.

"We are told that the imperial physicians have done their utmost," one said, "yet like a ragged cloak on a beggar's back, a doleful malady still clings about our ruler."

"And more alarming yet," the dihqan said, "a rumor reached us only yesterday that Dahak, a monstrous serpent with three heads, has broken free from his prison on Mount Damavand. There he was chained long ago by our ancestors; but now, hiding in dark groves and behind great rocks, it is said, he advances steadily upon the capital at Bishapur."

"To what purpose, do you think?" Balakrama asked.

"Why surely to break the emperor's will by seizing, if he can, the glorious standard of imperial power, the leathern apron of the blacksmith, Kawa. It was he who raised the rebellion by which Dahak was conquered long ago. But if this new rumor is true, the evil serpent, now wild with freedom, wishes to possess the standard's power and make himself the emperor."

"What can be done?" asked Rajahsingha. "Have the imperial guards been sent to destroy him?"

"Many times," the dihqan said, "for the stories about him have been as numerous as ravens in the summer. But none have found the serpent, though his three heads are each as large as a lion's, and his body moves but slowly along the earth."

"What more can be done?" asked Rajahsingha.

"We do not know," the dihqan said, "but some days ago, an elderly traveler, who stopped here but a single night, spoke on the matter.

" 'Dahak cannot be conquered by the sword of a palace guard,' he said, 'for this treacherous serpent with a flick of the long tongue in any of his heads can cause a man to fall into a sleep as deep as the ocean for a night and a day.'

" 'How then may he be overcome?' I asked.

" 'Dahak's power lies in the three long necks which

support his three great heads,' the old man said.

"His eyes were shining with excitement, bright as new moons, while he went on.

" 'Only if these be twisted together like three strands in one cord can Dahak be subdued. Then he would be weakened and the imperial bird could carry him away.'

"This bird," the dihqan said to the princes, "is she who is called the Simurgh. Preening her long tail-feathers of blue, green and rose, she sits day and night on the roof of the palace and guards our emperor."

The dihqan looked thoughtful.

"It seems," he said, "that the old traveler has described the sole way to thwart the wiley Dahak from his purpose; but this appears so difficult, we can only hope that the tale of the monster's escape is simply rumor."

The three brothers had given each other quick glances while the dihqan was speaking.

When he finished, Balakrama said, "I am with you in that hope, but tell us more about the old man with whom you spoke. He may be one for whom we seek."

"As I remember," the headman said, "he was dressed much as a farmer in a brown tunic and dark trousers. On his right arm he wore an iron bracelet incised with a design of stars. Those in the house where he stayed said he slept but little and mumbled in his sleep; but by morning he seemed well rested, and never had they seen anyone with brighter eyes."

"How like Aphoenicius!" Vijayo said. "Pray, which way did he go as he left this village?"

"Now that leads me to relate a strange thing," the

dihqan said, "for although he spoke his farewells and thanks, none of us saw him setting out."

"How then can we follow him," Rajahsingha said to his brothers, "when there are as many directions as there are winds to blow in them?"

To this all agreed, and soon the gathering dispersed. The next morning before departing, the princes thanked their host profusely and attempted to give him a jewelled ring in gratitude for his hospitality, but he graciously refused it.

"Our village has been more than rewarded by the honor of your visit," he said. "For you who have recovered the Mirror of Justice are like stars making bright the lanes of our small village."

"You give us too much praise," Balakrama said, "but at least allow us to present you with a token of our friendship."

Saying this, he handed to the chief villager a peacock feather he had brought from India. It was the very same one he had used for protection against Asura.

"May it serve you well as once it shielded me," said Balakrama. "And if ever we can be of assistance to you or to your people, pray, send it to us."

At these words, the dihqan of Kuhabad bowed very low and accepted the green-blue feather. Then the three princes continued on their way to the capital of the Emperor Vahram.

The young men crossed valleys with woodlands of sycamore and poplar trees, growing by mountain streams. They climbed many high and rocky hills. And at last they reached Bishapur, the capital.

There they first sought Zahmes, the Grand Keeper of the Royal Orders, of whom they inquired concerning the emperor and to whom they turned over the Mirror of Justice. Also, after revealing their royal names, and telling him that they were sons of the King of Serendip, the brothers said that provided their father approved, a marriage had been arranged between Rajahsingha and Parvathi, the fair young queen of India.

As soon as this news reached the emperor, he asked Zahmes to bring the princes before him. The brothers were shocked and dismayed to see how much their friend had changed.

Although the emperor was still a young man, his face was creased with worry, drawn with grief, and pale with illness. Only by a great effort could he speak to the princes at all, and even then, was not able to raise his head.

"Ill as I am," he said, "for you my gratitude has flowered like the peach blossom, which seems with its beauty to thank the sunlight and the rain. I rejoice that you have so gloriously succeeded in the purpose of your journey, and I am glad to welcome you as sons of my old friend, the King of Serendip."

The three princes bowed low, and the emperor continued to speak.

"In spite of this pleasure, however," he said, "Your Highnesses find me exceedingly ill. Indeed, unless your genius can discover a cure, I believe I shall die very soon."

The brothers bowed again, and Balakrama said, "Our hearts are grieved to see you thus. It will be our earnest endeavor to help if we can. May we ask whence came this malady which has driven the light and joy from Your Imperial Majesty's eyes?"

Questioned in this way, Vahram spoke sadly to the princes of Deliramma, and told how, in a moment of fury, he had caused her to be driven into the wilderness. At this point his eyes filled with tears of such bitter regret that he covered his face with his hands.

"I know not how I could have been so cruel, even in anger, to one so fair," he said. "My palace guards have searched for her in vain. Surely by now some fierce beast must have consumed her, and behold the wretched plight to which I am reduced."

When the three princes heard this tale, their hearts were filled with pity, both for Deliramma, whom they had never seen, and for the Emperor Vahram whose suffering was plainly visible.

"Since Your Majesty asks our counsel," Balakrama said. "permit us to withdraw and consult among ourselves, so that we may discover what we should advise."

Granted this request, the three brothers left the emperor's apartment; and as soon as possible, Vijayo sought an audience with the Princess Purandocht. She was robed in white with a girdle of gold, and looked as fair as the narcissus; but her delicate face was drawn with worry.

"I rejoice to see you," she said, "but all my happiness is dimmed by my brother's illness. Not only is His Imperial Majesty sadly ailing, but word has reached us that Dahak, a serpent of evil with three horrible heads, has broken out of the cave in which he once was chained. Even now, it is said, he approaches the capital. No doubt he wishes to wrest from my brother the Imperial Standard and even the golden throne itself."

Here she wrung her hands, and tears flowed down her cheeks.

"Surely you can help us," she said. "I have long been living with that hope."

When Vijayo repeated this to Balakrama and Rajahsingha, they were very solemn and went immediately to a window to look at the Imperial Standard. It flew from a tall pole in the great courtyard of the palace—a leathern apron, such as any blacksmith might use, but fastened by golden cords. At the foot of the pole were three palace guards.

Higher than the flag itself, on a corner of the roof, the princes also saw the emperor's great bird, the old Simurgh. She had long talons and was preening her feathers which glowed with colors: blue like the sky, green like the grass, and rose like a sunset.

Seeing the Imperial Standard guarded thus, the three brothers next consulted among themselves for some way to relieve the suffering of the Emperor Vahram.

"Finding a remedy for an affliction of the heart is not so easy as finding a stray camel," Balakrama said.

"Nor uncovering an ugly plot," said Vijayo.

"Nor facing the Fearsome Hand," added Rajahsingha.

All day the brothers walked up and down in their fine palace apartments and thought and thought without success. When night came, they slept uneasily; and finally with the dawn, they decided to ride up to the top of a nearby mountain, where they might be away from other people and the noise of the town to think in peace.

Here they dismounted and looked out upon the valley and trees below. They thought of the great capital with its luxurious palace and grieving emperor, and they thought of the small village of Kuhabad with its few comforts but many smiles.

Finally Balakrama said, "Since His Imperial Majesty is ill with sorrow, perhaps a taste of happiness would lift his spirits."

After weighing this thought with care, the three brothers agreed upon a plan, though with scant hope of much success. Then they returned to the palace and asked to see the emperor again.

When they were admitted to his presence, they bowed very low; and Balakrama said, "All around this capital are many valleys with prospects of exquisite beauty and wholesome air. In order to recover Your Majesty's health, we suggest the building of a palace in each of seven different places of this kind.

"Let them be pleasing in design and handsome in appointments. When they are completed, visit a different one each day for seven days."

"Besides this," the second prince said, "we recommend that as soon as orders are given for the palaces to be built, ambassadors be sent into seven of the greatest countries of the world to invite here seven princesses, daughters of mighty monarchs. Let each of them, with her maids in waiting, visit in a different palace to delight Your Imperial Majesty with royal conversation."

"Finally," Prince Rajahsingha said, "we respectfully suggest that Your Majesty ask to come hither the greatest storyteller in each of the seven largest cities of this land. Let one of these visit in each palace, so that the telling of stories may help to drive away the unhappiness which long has made Your Majesty so ill."

By this time the emperor was in such great despair over all the prescriptions that were not helping, and was so full of confidence in the wisdom of the three princes of Serendip, that he immediately decided to accept their counsel. He ordered his architects to commence work at once on seven palaces, each to be situated in a spot with a pleasant prospect and healthful air.

Also he commanded seven ambassadors to depart for audiences with seven mighty monarchs, to ask that each permit one of his fairest daughters to visit in the land of Persia. Finally, word was sent to the seven largest cities of the empire saying that the Emperor Vahram desired the services of the greatest storyteller living in each.

All of these commands were executed with remarkable speed. So expert were the emperor's architects and builders, that the seven palaces were completed at the same time and with incredible swiftness. Each was magnificent and pleasingly different from the others in both design and furnishings. Moreover, every one was filled with enough rice, wheat, and other provisions to last the imperial court for several months, in case the emperor should wish to prolong his visit in any one of them.

Hardly were the palaces ready when the ambassadors returned from distant lands with seven princesses, all fair like the moment of dawn, gentle in speech, and royally accomplished.

As each arrived with her ladies in waiting, splendid horses, and handsome equipage, crowds thronged into the streets to see the bright processions. People waved in welcome and called out words of gratitude to the fair maidens, who had traveled so far to help the ailing emperor.

After each princess reached the capital, the three brothers sought out the ambassador who had been sent to bring her and asked if he had noted any signs of Dahak, the evil serpent. None of them, however, had the least news of the monster until the seventh one arrived.

"We did not see him," this ambassador said, "but when we were still twenty parasangs from here, we heard a great hissing, which sounded like a mighty wind, and indeed a storm arose. Fearful that Dahak had caused this disturbance and that he might appear at any moment to frighten the princess, we hurried on."

Soon the seven storytellers also arrived. Young and popular, they, too, were welcomed by great throngs in the imperial city. Questioned by the princes concerning Dahak, none had aught to report until the seventh reached Bishapur.

This one said, "Ten parasangs away as I traveled hither, I saw at dusk, a grove of sycamores. Entwined along the trunk of one of these trees there seemed to be something dark like a thick coil of black rope. It had three heads, and from the mouth of each issued fiery sparks. Perhaps there I saw Dahak, but I did not dare to stop."

The princes were much disturbed by these reports. They informed Zahmes, and he sent out the palace guards again and again to look for the great serpent, but nowhere did they find him.

Little rain had fallen that year, and it was near the end of summer. In the farmlands beyond the city, the struggling wheat plants were so dry that they seemed to wail in complaint as the evening winds rustled through their stiff stalks. Many of the people in Bishapur were fearful for the harvest, but they greeted the visitors with smiles.

When at last all was in readiness, a day was fixed for the emperor to travel to the first palace. On the night before, the three princes were making ready to accompany him. It was late, but they had not yet gone to bed when they heard three curious thuds as if as many men had fallen to the ground. The sounds came from the courtyard.

The brothers hurried to a window. Outside, the moonlight touched everything with a veil of silver. By this light the princes were able to see the pole bearing the Imperial Standard, and to their horror they could clearly discern a huge serpent entwined about it. The serpent had three great heads, each emitting

bursts of flame, as its body spiraled slowly upwards. Below, slumped to the ground, lay the three guards.

The three princes hurried to the courtyard. There, hardly breathing, they hid themselves in a dark shadow.

Dahak, with his heads thrust out in three directions, continued to slither higher and higher up the pole, with slow but steady speed. Finally, placing the end of his tail on the ground, he pulled upward on the pole with his strong coils until it was uprooted and the Imperial Standard fell with a dull flop to the earth.

So amazed were the three princes that for a few moments they could only watch and feel a fear within them they had not known before.

Then they saw another extraordinary thing. Dahak's great body unwound itself from the lowered pole. Soon he held it in three different places by the three mouths of his three great heads. Raising the Standard, slowly, he began to crawl off with the pole over his back. And moving slowly with it, was the blacksmith's apron.

Now was the moment to act. While grasping the pole in his mouths, Dahak could not attack with his dart-like tongues. And the princes felt sure he was too greedy for power to drop the pole. In a long bound Rajahsingha jumped upon his tail. Balakrama seized the pole near the Standard. Vijayo grabbed the pole at the other end.

While the three heads still held onto the pole, the two older brothers walked swiftly around and around. So the long necks were twisted till they looked like the strands of a giant rope. This done, the princes could remove the Standard to a safe place and bind Dahak's great necks together with the golden cords which had held the apron of the blacksmith, Kawa.

Only then did the serpent slump to the earth. His greedy heads, at last relaxed their hold on the long pole, and the princes bent to pick it up. Then the powerful Simurgh flew down from the roof of the palace, her great wings like dark fans spread out in the night.

Grasping the enormous snake in her tremendous claws, she flew up into the air with a loud screech. The princes saw her circling off with the silver moonlight on her back while sparks of fire dropped from the three wide mouths of Dahak.

The palace guards who had fallen at the foot of the pole still lay as if asleep. Other guards, awakened by the screech of the imperial bird, now ran into the courtyard. When they learned what had happened, they mounted their horses to follow the old Simurgh and her prey.

By early dawn, they returned and said that after flying in great circles, she had dropped Dahak on a nearby peak. Here the guards had speedily loaded him with fetters and chained him once more in a mountain cave. As for the three men who had been put to sleep by the tongues in the three great heads, they did not wake up until the following night.

When the emperor heard how Dahak had been conquered, he was again full of gratitude towards his three friends from Serendip.

"As long as you reside in my empire," he said, "yours shall be the right of access to my Imperial Person without announcement. By this permission I trust you will understand the depths of my gratitude and the confidence I place in Your Royal Highnesses."

Then with apparently more spirit than he had shown before, Vahram prepared to visit the first palace. For this occasion he had himself clothed in a garment of golden cloth and wore a cap with threads of gold and jewelled ornaments in a design of crescents and peacocks.

All of his courtiers and the three princes of Serendip were similarly dressed in robes of golden cloth. Even the bridles of the horses were decked with rosettes of gold ribbon, which shone in the sunlight like bright stars against their dark heads.

Although the imperial procession to the first palace was as magnificent as the people had ever seen, the emperor himself was so weak that he had to be carried by litter. His short dark beard was combed and neatly curled, but the long illness had made his eyes dull and his face pale as a white rose.

When his subjects saw this, they cried out, "Ah!" in pity, and then in hope, "May Your Majesty's health soon be restored. Long live Our Emperor!"

Warmed by their sympathy and encouraged by their hope, Vahram finally arrived at the first palace. Since he could not sit up without suffering, he asked to be placed on a couch. Resting in the great courtyard, he admired the graceful arches of the palace and the garden it surrounded. Here were newly-planted trees of peach and apricot, also a wide pool reflecting the flight of mountain birds.

Before long, a warm and gusty breeze sprang up which made the trees sway like dancers. The three princes, hearing the sound of hissing in the wind, feared that Dahak, even though chained in a cave, had blown up a great storm. So they urged His Imperial Majesty to go inside for safety.

The interior of the palace and its furnishings were ornamented with fine gold. This in turn was inlaid with African diamonds and pearls from cool ledges of the Indian Ocean.

In the great hall the three brothers saw the first princess as she came forth to welcome the emperor. Gracefully gowned in cloth of gold, she entered the hall to the sound of stringed instruments, which were played by her twelve ladies in waiting. Each was so accomplished that the music was full of enchantment.

With a charming smile, the princess bowed to the ailing emperor and said, "My heart is distressed to see Your Majesty so ill, but also rejoices to welcome Your Imperial Splendor into this abode of magnificence and serenity."

Vahram, pleased to be greeted by so lovely and gracious a lady, said, "I doubt not that Your Royal Highness' sympathy and courtesy will soon have a happy effect upon my health. With all my heart, therefore, I thank Your Highness for traveling far from your own land to aid in my recovery."

After that the princess and the emperor talked for a long while. They exchanged many agreeable remarks.

Some of hers made Vahram, sad as he was, smile just a little. Then the royal visitor and all of her ladies in waiting withdrew, and His Imperial Majesty summoned the first storyteller.

A young man, who knew more tales than anyone else in his home city, arrived and bowed very low.

When Vahram signified he had permission to speak, the storyteller said, "It grieves me sorely to see Your Majesty so ill, but I hope the adventure I can relate will beguile Your Imperial sorrow and speed Your Majesty back to health."

The emperor, who was passionately fond of stories, said, "I have no doubt that in some measure you will succeed, for a skillful tale, well told, has power to move the heart and elevate the mind. Pray, therefore, proceed at once."

Thus commanded, the first storyteller began an account of strange happenings. Not only did the emperor listen with pleasure, but also the three princes of Serendip. They resolved to remember what they heard so that some day they might be able to tell the same story to their father, King Jaiya, whom they longed so much to see again.

The next morning the ground trembled, the sky was dark, and the wind was blowing harder than before. Questioned by the princes, Zahmes reported that although Dahak could not escape from the cave, he was standing in chains at its entrance, shaking the earth with his thumping tail and filling the valley with hissing winds in his anger and disappointment.

"I have just given orders," Zahmes said, "for the

guards to put heavier chains upon him and to heap up a pile of earth in front of the cave. All this will take time, however, so we may expect the trembling of the earth and the storm he has raised to continue for several days."

Vahram heard this news but nevertheless decided to follow the original plan. So once more, the imperial party started forth, with the emperor again being carried on a litter. This time, however, he was able to raise his head just a little so that people along the roads, even from a distance, could see his pale face.

The second palace was hung with purple tapestries, the third was made of rosy marble, and fourth inlaid with shining onyx. As for the fifth, it was bright with paintings; and the sixth was panelled with fragrant cedar.

All of these, however, were surpassed by the seventh, for it was surrounded with flowering gardens, ornamented with sculptures on rock cliffs, and situated on a lake. Here teal, heron, and other water birds came to drink, though they were battered now by the stormy winds that still blew as strong as ocean gales.

The seventh princess, too, was the most beautiful of them all. Her hair was as dark as the sky at night. Her eyes were as bright as new moons, and her conversation sweet as the sound of birds upon awakening.

And of all the stories he heard in the seven palaces, Vahram liked best those of the seventh storyteller. His were full of brave heroes, strange beasts, and many surprises.

Indeed, so pleased was the emperor by the seventh

palace, the princess, and the storyteller that he decided to prolong his visit. Although still rather weak and somewhat sad, the ruler was now able to stand alone and even to walk unaided. The three princes, whose plan had succeeded better than they had expected, were delighted.

One day, to divert His Majesty still further, Vijayo began teaching him to play chess, a game which the prince had learned in India. At the same time, Balakrama and Rajahsingha were making a new song.

Before they had time to sing it, however, an imperial servant came into the room, carrying a peacock feather.

Bowing humbly, he handed the feather to Balakrama and said, "A man from Kuhabad, who came here on foot, asked me to give you this."

Alarmed at the sight of the token, the oldest prince said, "And pray, what more did he say?"

"He murmured something about a great disaster," the servant reported. "Then in haste he ran back in the direction from which he had come."

"We will go at once to Kuhabad," Balakrama said, "for our friends there must be in need."

With the emperor's permission, they left immediately upon swift horses. The wind was blowing now with such wild strength they had to lean against it in order to move forward. Moreover, the earth trembled and shook beneath them. But they rode on swiftly.

As for the song which Balakrama and Rajahsingha had made, it was now forgotten. A long time would pass before they would think of singing it again, but this is what it was:

PANTOUM FOR THE SEVENTH PALACE

A princess makes a palace bright,
A storyteller makes one gay
To cure an emperor by delight
As Vahram's smiles slip out to play.

A storyteller makes one gay
With enchantments learned from long ago
As Vahram's smiles slip out to play
Though mountain storming winds may blow.

With enchantments learned from long ago
To cure an emperor by delight,
Though mountain storming winds may blow,
A princess makes a palace bright.

THE
Sad Disaster

In spite of the gales blowing hard upon them, snapping at their cloaks and even tugging the reins in their hands, and in spite of the ground shaking beneath them, the three princes rode steadfastly across the valleys and along the steep mountain roads to Kuhabad. As they drew near, suddenly, the sharp winds and trembling of the earth abated, but in the cloudy air was an odor of smoke as heavy as musk.

Abruptly then they came to a clearing high on the Persian mountainside from which they could look down upon the valley where the village lay. Immediately they saw that a great fire had swept across the farmlands. It appeared also that the tremors in the earth had severely damaged the houses.

Roofs of the once neat homes were fallen in, walls were dark with soot, and bundles of hay formerly stored beside them had been burnt up. Where wheat had been growing in the fields, there were only charred remains. It was as if night, fleeing from the blaze of morning, had dropped a gigantic cloak upon the valley floor.

The people walked with slow steps about their ruined village or huddled in its center. Moreover, even from their distant height, the three brothers could hear the wails of small children.

At the sight, the sound, and the thought of the suffering of their friends of Kuhabad, the hearts of the three princes were filled with pity. Tears welled up in their eyes and poured down their cheeks, at first in small drops, then in flowing streams. These gathered in a small pool, filling a rocky basin.

Indeed, the three brothers were so overcome with compassion for the people of Kuhabad that at first they could not move; but finally they hurried down the mountainside to learn what might be done for their afflicted friends. As they rode, the villagers saw them coming and a party of elders, headed by the dihqan, walked swiftly towards them.

"Behold, Noble Friends," the headman said, "you see our homes in ruins and our crops destroyed."

"In this dark moment we are grieving with you," Balakrama said. "Pray, tell us what brought here so much misfortune."

The dihqan said, "First we saw the Simurgh. She

flew above our village bearing in her claws an enormous creature, looking like the descriptions we have heard of the serpent Dahak. It had three long necks twisted together. On the end of each was a head of lion size with a wide mouth from which dropped glowing sparks."

He waved his hand toward the burnt fields and continued.

"When they fell onto our farmlands, long dry from lack of rain, fire sprang up instantly. We tried to stamp it out, but to no avail, for there followed a great wind which lifted the flames from one stalk to another, while smoke and sparks raced through our village like angry beasts, and fierce winds beat down upon our houses. Then the earth shook under our homes so that walls cracked and roofs fell."

"Has any person been lost in this disaster?" asked Balakrama.

"Two are missing, whom we have sought in vain," the dihqan said. "Both came to us as strangers and stayed among us but a short time. One was the old man of whom we spoke when last you were here. Not until after the fire did I learn he had come back the night before and stayed with a farmer on the edge of the village. Next evening he could not be found, and again none of us saw him leave."

Balakrama looked at his two brothers. Once more had Aphoenicius, like a shadow, slipped away from them.

"And the other person?" the oldest prince said.

"A young woman," the dihqan said. "She had been

found nearby in the mountains, half-starved and very ill. Our women nursed her back to health. We did not know her name nor may we ever. It seems that she, vainly trying with us to put out the fire, may have perished in it."

Looking around, Vijayo said, "The plight of Kuhabad is sad indeed. Please accept such small provisions or foodstuff as we carry and let us know your needs so that we may inform His Imperial Majesty, the emperor."

Accompanied by the dihqan, the brothers walked through the village. The people thronged around to thank them for coming, while the princes, with deep concern, inquired about their losses.

Then they said to the headman, "We have heard of a shorter way to return, a route to the west. Over that way we shall speed quickly back to the emperor and tell him of what has happened. Have no doubt he will immediately send you aid."

"We are grateful for your coming," the dihqan said. "When you travel forth, may you go with speed and safety. I ask only one thing: Beware of the marshlands on your route, for the Bottomless Pool lies in their midst."

The princes thanked him for his warning, mounted their horses, and set out for the seventh palace. Before leaving the border of the village, they went around a small grove of trees which had escaped the fire, and ascended a small blackened hill.

Looking down when he reached the crest, Balakrama suddenly saw something which made him stop. Turning back, he called to his brothers.

"Look!" he said, as he dismounted quickly.

On the sooty earth, pierced with the blackened remains of stalks of wheat, something long and round was shining in the sunlight.

The oldest prince stooped over as his brothers rode up to him and leapt from their horses. What Balakrama had found was a bright cylinder clutched in a charred hand. This was on the end of an arm which disappeared in a heap of ashes, but around this arm the princes saw a bracelet with a design of stars, still visible under a coat of soot.

"Poor Aphoenicius," Vijayo said. "We have missed him again and again, and now he has perished in this fire."

"Still holding the silver case," Rajahsingha said. He picked it up and handed it to Balakrama.

As he did so, the brothers saw that it was sealed at one end, but open at the other. The oldest prince, his fingers clumsy with excitement, reached inside and drew forth the remains of a yellowed scroll, badly charred. Unnoticed by the princes, the cylinder fell to the ground as Balakrama carried what had been its contents down the hill to the shade of the grove of trees.

Here, despite their urgent errand for the village, they sat down, and Balakrama unrolled the faded parchment of which the scroll was made. Then, like a piece of driftwood on a shore overtaken by tidal waters, the princes were swept into a vast sea of disappointment. What had been found was only a fragment of the scroll, cut off abruptly. On it was written just the beginning of a poem.

This is what the brothers read:

Death To Dragons

Though the treasure saline be,
You will not scoop it from the sea,
And often from the sight is hidden
Such magic not by wishes bidden.
One may seek but cannot borrow
This mystery lying close to sorrow.

There was no more writing, for the rest of the scroll had been burned in the fire. Its remains were now ashes in the hands of the oldest prince. The three brothers were plunged into further gloom.

"After so long a search," said Rajahsingha, "we have found only the lines we already knew."

"So small a part is useless," Vijayo said, "And the whole formula of *Death to Dragons* in a hundred lines is lost forever. What shall we say to our father, and how may we ever step again onto the shore of Serendip?"

For a few moments the three princes, their hopes banished, sat quite still.

Finally, Balakrama said, "All we can do is inform our father of what has happened. Let us send him this fragment and also the silver case. Then although he will see thereby how miserably we have failed, he will know it is useless to search any more."

So, weary and discouraged, the three brothers rose

to return to the spot on the hill where Balakrama had let the cylinder fall. As they looked up, it could still be seen. Then, however, a very strange thing happened.

The center of the pile of ashes, in the place where Aphoenicius had fallen, began to move. As it did so, the princes saw a bright gleam. Then slowly emerging from the heap came a golden bird. It had eyes like fire and shining feathers, which flashed in the sunlight.

"Look! look!" said Balakrama. "Aphoenicius lives again in the shape of yonder bird."

"So it truly seems," Vijayo said, thinking that never had he seen a feathered thing so beautiful.

"And what will he do now?" said Rajasingha.

The three princes hurried forward to pick up the silver case, but to their amazement, before they reached it, the golden bird had seized it in his beak. As if in search of something, he flew around and around. Then he headed for the mountain clearing where the three brothers earlier that day had looked down upon the village. Here he alighted beside the pool of princes' tears, shed in compassion for the people of Kuhabad.

Into this, the astonished young men saw him dip the cylinder of silver. Finally, after it had apparently been filled with their own tears, they saw the golden bird, still carrying the case in his beak, fly away to the east, higher and higher, like a great eagle, until he was out of sight.

"It is good to know that he still lives," Balakrama said, "but alas, not only is the full formula now lost forever, but we do not have even the silver cylinder to show our father."

Extremely downhearted, the princes once more took to their horses and rode up into the mountains. So dejected were they that it seemed as if they carried the whole sky upon their shoulders.

They rode along the upland roads for nearly two parasangs. Each was lost in his own thoughts, until suddenly through a thick grove of trees there came the sound of a woman's cry. It was full of such terror that they turned aside immediately to seek the cause of the distress. The way led down a small path, declining steeply.

After riding as fast as they could down the narrow passage between the trees, the princes came to a clearing and saw that the path circled on towards some marshy land. Along it ran a young woman, uttering screams which pierced the air. Close behind her followed a wild boar, snorting and showing his sharp teeth.

Rajahsingha at once raced ahead of his brothers and lifted his voice in a mighty shout. Abruptly the boar stopped. Then he swung around and charged uphill at the youngest prince. But when the two older brothers caught up with Rajahsingha, the great beast, as if suddenly frightened by the sight of so many men and their horses, dashed quickly off the path. He plunged off into the marshy ground with the youngest prince in pursuit.

The way was so rough with fallen branches and great boulders, that Rajahsingha could not gain upon the boar, and the animal plunged deep into the marshland. Then all at once he floundered about and disappeared, as if the shallow waters of the marsh had swallowed him completely.

"Come back! Come back!" shouted the two older brothers to the youngest. "That must be the Bottomless Pool. Come back, or you will perish like the boar."

Rajahsingha, who in the excitement of chasing the animal had forgotten the dihqan's warning about a dangerous marshland, came to a sudden stop. His brothers had called just in time. With some difficulty then he turned around and went back up to the path. Here all the princes fastened the reins of their horses to trees and walked to where the young woman had dropped to the ground.

"The boar has perished in yonder marsh," Rajahsingha said. "Have no fear of him, but we implore you to go no farther along this way, or you too may disappear in the Bottomless Pool."

The young woman lifted her head and said, "Then surely you have saved my life, for either I should have fallen therein or been torn to pieces by the boar."

She looked up as she spoke, and the princes saw that although her clothes were old and torn, her face was as fair as a round, bright moon.

"Pray, tell us," Balakrama said, "where your home is, and how you come to be wandering here alone?"

"Alas," the young woman said, "I have no home and long have wandered alone. For a while I was sheltered and fed by the kind people of Kuhabad, but they have suffered a great disaster and have not food enough for themselves. So, not to be a burden upon them, I have fled into the mountain wilderness once more, and again make my way alone."

When the princes heard her tale, they were full of astonishment. But a moment later each made the same guess as to why she wandered alone. Balakrama spoke first.

"Alas," he said, "I see that one in a wilderness may walk alone, while another sighs in a palace surrounded by people."

"What do you mean?" the young woman asked rising to her feet.

"Only that I know an exalted person who lives in a palace," said Balakrama, "yet every day he sighs with regret and grief. This is because in a moment of anger he had a fair young lady, whom he loved, driven alone and forlorn into a dark forest. Now he wishes nothing more than to ask her forgiveness and restore her to his full protection."

With a look of great surprise, the young woman said, "These words almost stir my heart to hope. Pray, tell me who this personage may be."

"I speak of the Emperor Vahram," Balakrama said. "For many months he has been ill over the loss of one we have never seen, called Deliramma."

The young woman sat down on the trunk of an overturned tree near the place where she had been standing.

"So am I called," she said, "but in truth I do not know my real name. I was discovered when an infant in the land of India by the leader of a caravan."

The three princes bowed very low. "If you are willing, it will be our great joy," they said, "to bring you back to His Imperial Majesty who has longed so much to see you."

"Then I shall go with you gladly," Deliramma said, "but before I do," she added, looking at Rajahsingha, "allow me to give you this, for it was your daring and your kindness that saved my life today."

At these words, she took from her arm something that gleamed in the afternoon sunlight.

"Take this infant necklace, which I have worn as a bracelet," she said. "It is all that I have from my former estate, but I wish it to be yours."

When Rajahsingha saw what she had placed in his hands, he was nearly overwhelmed. The necklace was made with tiny links in the shape of crowns.

Bowing low, he said, "My gratitude towards you is boundless as the wind, but I cannot accept a treasure so important. Besides, I am more than blessed by the message that it brings."

He turned to his brothers and said,"Twice fortunate are we today, for we have found not only the beauteous Deliramma, but also the lost sister of my beloved Queen Parvathi."

Then looking at the young woman, he said, "Surely you are none other than the Princess Padmini."

At first the young woman could not believe the news her ears received and she asked the princes many questions. They told her what they had learned in India about her history: the abduction, the necklace with links in the shape of crowns, and the garment of pale blue silk, which she had been wearing when lost so long ago.

"The caravan leader, my foster father, has told me of this garment," she said, "so now I do believe you, but how can I express the joy I feel?"

"After the emperor hears our news," said Balakrama, "he will have all the trumpets of his empire blown to show his joy."

So, highly elated by thoughts of the gladness they were bringing to their friend, the three princes of Serendip, with the princess, continued on their way to the seventh palace. As they did so, they made this song:

PANTOUM FOR THE PRINCESS PADMINI

Let trumpets in delirium sound
Where boars are wilder than the gales.
Our precious Padmini is found
More beautiful than fairy tales.

Where boars are wilder than the gales
Upon a Persian mountainside
More beautiful than fairy tales,
Three princes to her rescue ride.

Upon a Persian mountainside
Our precious Padmini is found.
Three princes to her rescue ride;
Let trumpets in delirium sound.

THE

Golden Bird

As the three princes of Serendip and Princess Padmini rode on, the young men were filled with feelings strangely mixed. On the one hand, they rejoiced in the happy news they were bringing to the Emperor Vahram; on the other, they had many misgivings, because they had failed to find the formula of *Death of Dragons* before all but a tiny fragment of it had burned in the fire at Kuhabad.

When they neared the palace, Rajahsingha rode swiftly ahead of the others. This was not only to let Vahram know that his lost love, Deliramma, had been found, but also to see that all was in readiness to receive her as the Princess Padmini.

In haste to bring his news, the youngest prince was glad he had the privilege of entering the imperial apartments without waiting to be announced. Soon he stood before the emperor and found upon that ruler's face a look of great dismay and in his hands an opened letter.

"Alas," the emperor said to the prince, "even in this abode of gentle loveliness troubles come like swarms of gnats."

"What has happened?" asked Rajahsingha.

"I have here a letter," the emperor said, "from the merchant leader of the caravan which brought Deliramma to me. As her foster father, he asks to see his daughter again and comes hither on this very day. Now tell me, what message can I send him?"

The third prince bowed very low. "I respectfully suggest that Your Imperial Majesty dispatch word that he is welcome and, as he wishes, may see his foster child."

Vahram opened his eyes wide. "How may that be?"

"It is my joyful errand," replied the prince, "to inform you that she approaches even now with my older brothers."

Then he told the emperor not only of the manner in which she had been found but of her own true name and, in a few words, of how she had been befriended by the kind people of Kuhabad. Also he described the dire plight of the village.

When Vahram learned that his beloved was coming back, he rose looking as strong and well as a young lion. Quickly he called the Grand Keeper of the Royal Orders, and, in words that seemed to tumble over each other in haste and happiness, issued commands:

"My horse at once . . . the finest apartments for Her Royal Highness . . . every trumpet in joyful salute . . . And Kuhabad . . ."

A cloud of pity crossed his countenance.

He said, "Everything they need . . . The architects and builders of my seven palaces . . . Let them go to the village and rebuild at once. As for provisions, we have more than enough in the first six palaces . . . here, too. Send a great quantity."

He turned to Rajahsingha. "Pray, show me the way your brothers come with the princess. Let us waste no time."

At this, he hurried from the palace and flung himself on a swift horse as if he had never at all been ill. Rajahsingha led the way with Vahram at his side, followed by a troop of courtiers. So eager was the emperor, that soon he and Rajahsingha had left the others a long way behind.

The two rode swiftly for a distance of one parasang, and then Rajahsingha saw his brothers with the Princess Padmini coming around a curving path not far ahead. The late afternoon sun sent forth a great burst of glory while it set beyond a distant peak, and, as if aware of a moment too precious for sound, the mountain birds were silent. Rajahsingha heard only the hoofbeats of the horses.

When the two parties met, all dismounted quickly. The emperor, who had been in such haste to meet his beloved again, then hesitated a moment. As if fearing she might turn and run away, he approached her slowly.

But the princess ran forward to the emperor, fell on her knees, and bowed her face to the ground.

She said, "May I hope Your Imperial Majesty will pardon one who was once so thoughtless?"

Vahram said, "Is it possible that Your Royal Highness can forgive one who was once so harsh?"

Then without waiting for an answer, he took her hand and helped her rise while her tears of joy fell like gems, shining in the fiery light of the setting sun.

When they had all returned to the palace, the sound of trumpets commenced a great celebration. The princess was given splendid apartments and rich robes, suited to her station. And Prince Rajahsingha dispatched a letter to Queen Parvathi of India that she might rejoice, too, in the finding of her lost sister.

Once more there was music and feasting in the imperial palace and all across the land, in honor of the Emperor Vahram and the Princess Padmini, who would soon become his wife. Moreover the three brothers received many honors, gifts, and other signs of imperial gratitude.

The merchant of the caravan rejoiced to learn of the happiness and high estate of his foster daughter. Hearing how she had been sheltered by the people of Kuhabad, he undertook to transport thither in his caravan a great part of the provisions sent by the emperor to assist the people there. Thus the merchant was able to bring them word of the imperial gratitude for the kindness shown to Deliramma and also, as her foster father, to thank them on his own behalf.

As for the seven princesses, whose thoughtfulness and charm had helped the emperor, each of them, with the permission of the monarchs who were their fathers, consented in marriage to one of the seven storytellers. The royal ladies considered these artists to be princes among men, and loved them as much for their sensitive hearts as they admired them for their remarkable genius. Learning of this happy turn of events, the emperor, who had returned to his capital at Bishapur, was pleased to bestow titles of nobility upon all of the storytellers and gave to each couple one of his seven new palaces for a home.

The three princes rejoiced in the good fortune of their friends, even though their hearts were pierced like plump walnuts bored by hungry worms because of their own failure in the matter of *Death to Dragons.* So things stood for many a day until one morning a messenger from Serendip arrived.

"Welcome always is one who comes from our homeland," Balakrama said. "Though our hearts are heavy with disappointments, pray, tell us quickly what word you bring."

"Both sweet and sorrowful," the messenger replied. "I have no letter. Time did not permit me to wait for writing; yet now, alas, we have too much of time."

"Pray, speak the message clearly," said Balakrama. "Riddles only tease our patience."

"His Majesty, King Jaiya," said the messenger, "continues ill, and now permits me, nay has urged me, to find Your Royal Highnesses swiftly and say that desperately and daily he longs to see his sons. Therefore, because of the great love he bears you, and even though no word has reached him that more than a few lines have been found of that formula called *Death to Dragons,* his Majesty calls Your Highnesses home."

Although much concerned by their father's illness, the princes rejoiced at his command.

"Alas, for the happiness I read in your faces," the messenger said, "for I have sad news, also. The dragons in the seas about our homeland are now so numerous and, worse still, so bold, that no sailor dares put forth across those waters; no ship, therefore, sails upon them. Indeed, the passage which I made to travel here was the very last, and barely did I reach the shore."

"Pray, tell us more of this," Rajahsingha said.

"From lashings of the monsters' tails," said the messenger, "our sturdy ship turned nearly over. So dangerous was the passage, that all the sailors on it vowed they would not cross the strait again. Likeminded, too, were all the seamen whom I questioned on the coast of India."

As a sudden storm darkens a sunwashed day, his words cast a veil of gloom over the happiness of the three princes. Nevertheless, in response to King Jaiya's word, they planned to leave the land of Persia and at least start out towards their own country.

When the emperor heard this news, he gave permission for them to go. But it was only with great reluctance that he could part with the three young men who had done so much for his country and for him.

Gratefully, he pressed upon them quantities of jewels, fine brocades, and rare books from his own library as gifts for King Jaiya and themselves.

Moreover, as he had done when they had left to face the Fearsome Hand, he accompanied them as far as Kuhabad, now almost rebuilt. Here the emperor and the three young princes were welcomed by the dihqan and all the people. These expressed their thanks with great bouquets of wildflowers.

At last the princes bade farewell to the Emperor Vahram, and pushed on. After traveling for many days, they entered India and passed again through the high lands of the Cheras, where first they had heard of Aphoenicius. Then finally they reached a place on the shore opposite their own homeland.

As they looked out over the water, a fearful sight was there. The wide sea strait was so filled with dragons that one could be seen riding high on the crest of nearly every wave. Each had a long and scaly tail which thrashed up billowing foam behind him. All along the shore every ship had been drawn up on the beach, and sailors stood idly by shaking their heads in dismay.

"No wonder even the brave and hardy refuse to cross these waters," Balakrama said.

"Nevertheless, we must reach our father, now that he has called us home," Vijayo said.

"Then let us sail a ship ourselves," said Rajahsingha.

Thereupon, with the aid of the messenger who had accompanied them, the three princes found and purchased the last ship that had sailed from Serendip. It was a strong vessel with a high mast, a yellow sail, and oars as well; but all of the seamen who had arrived on board refused even to put it into the water again, nor could the three brothers find any other sailors willing to help.

"We must launch the ship ourselves," Balakrama said.

So the three princes, assisted by the messenger from Serendip, began to push the vessel toward the sea. Meanwhile a great throng of fierce dragons gathered in the water close to the shore.

Seeing this, the messenger said, "Your Royal Highnesses, of what use will it be to launch this ship into the water? The instant we do so, the dragons will tear it to pieces and swallow us, too. Then who will see King Jaiya as his tears fall and double in abundance?"

"We do not command you to join us," Rajahsingha said, "but our father calls us to him, and for us there is no choice but to dare the passage."

At this the messenger, with both relief and fear upon his face, drew back while the three princes continued in their efforts. Nighttime came, and still the brothers strove, working until the ship was in the water. Then with their horses, led over some rough planks, they went on board.

Hardly had they poled the vessel from the shore, however, than a bold dragon clamped his jaws about the bow. Another leapt up out of the waves higher than the top of the mast.

The horses, lying down with their feet bound together to keep them safe, threw back their heads in fright. They rolled up their eyes, and their neighs of terror filled the salty air.

The three princes saw that the leaping dragon was the king of monsters in the sea. Against the moon's bright light was the outline of a crown upon his head, and on his body not only shining scales but weblike wings as well.

Each time he rose from the sea, the creature's dripping sides glistened with water. Then at the crest of one leap, he spread out his wings and, instead of returning to the waves, flew round and round above them.

The brothers were looking at the dragon in amazement, when another surprising sight came into view. Winging out of the darkness and across the stream of moonlight, dipped a great bird. Its eyes were like fire, and it carried something shiny in its beak.

For a moment the bird hovered above the ship. Then suddenly it dipped so low that the princes could see fall, from the container it held, a single drop of liquid. As soon as the drop reached the sea, the dragons near the ship slipped under the water.

Even with the light of the moon, the night was too dark to see very far; but since the monsters close by had disappeared, the three brothers hurriedly hoisted sail. Thus they set out through the seas for Serendip.

Overhead all along their way, the dragon king circled in the air. Instead of molesting the princes, however, he flew around and around as if in search of his subjects.

The three brothers, wondering at their unexpected good fortune, but fearing the arrival of more dragons

at any moment, managed to continue across the strait and reached Serendip before the dawn. In all their course they saw no monsters of the sea except the dragon king.

He pursued them until after they had anchored their ship and were disembarking with their horses. Then he gave a piercing shriek, and rising higher and higher, he flew off ahead of them in the direction of their home city, Anuradhapura.

As they started in the same direction, the three brothers, even in the faint light before dawn, could see that the growing things about them all looked dry and stiff. Passing villages they heard the cries of little children waking from sleep, but even when the approaching day spread a fan of rosy light in the east, no birds sang. Everything seemed strangely silent except the sound made by the galloping feet of the horses.

When the sun came up, round and golden, the princes neared the farmhouse where they had stopped and asked for water to drink just before they departed from Serendip. Balakrama felt a sudden pounding of his heart. Coming forth from the doorway of the house was a young woman, graceful as a jasmine vine stirred by a summer's wind.

In an instant he saw that she was Podihamine, the same whose image he had long and tenderly carried in his heart. At that moment, however, the dragon king reappeared high in the sky. Headlong, he dove toward the very spot where the young girl stood. His scales shone with the colors of green seaweed and old bronze. Like sapphires and emeralds were the jewels of his crown, blazing in the sunlight.

Unarmed, the oldest prince leapt from his horse and rushed fearlessly at the great monster. A moment later, his two brothers did the same. But in grappling with the slimy wings and tail of the dragon king, the princes felt themselves grow suddenly weak. It was as if all the rivers of their strength flowed from them into the fierce and ugly beast. His long tongue greedily licked the unfortunate Podihamine and his claws reached out for her. With a scream she crumpled and sank to the earth.

The brothers could hardly keep their feet on the ground. With little effect they grasped and tugged at the writhing monster.

As their hope for success waned, a shadow passed over. Glancing up, the princes saw, in the glory of the morning sunlight, the bird of the night before. His wings were spread and now the brothers could plainly see that he held in his beak a cylinder of silver. It could be none other than Aphoenicius.

From the cylinder, as he dipped for a moment into their sight, he let fall a single drop of liquid which landed upon the head of the dragon king. At this, the royal beast was caught up in a dark cloud by the wind, blown across the land, and dropped far out towards the sea.

As for Podihamine, with eyes closed, she lay unmoving on the ground. Her scream, however, had brought her father, mother, and neighbors running to her side. They gathered around as Balakrama took her hand and spoke to her softly; and the girl, unharmed but still fearful, opened her eyes.

When she saw that the dragon had vanished, she rose to thank the brave young men who had come to her rescue. In this moment she recognized that they were the three travelers she had seen, so long before.

Balakrama wanted to stay and talk with the fair Podihamine, but he was also in great haste to see his father. So, promising to return, he mounted his horse; and the three continued on their way to Anuradhapura.

After journeying for some time, the princes found themselves one morning before daylight approaching the great capital city. Taking a way which led towards the south and east, they rode between thick forests. Here they heard the trumpeting of bullfrogs and the familiar call of cicadas. After being so long away, even these seemed like music to the three brothers.

Then finally the capital city lay before them in the early light of dawn. They saw again the great Gold Dust Dagoba, where flower offerings always lay. These seemed few from what they now remembered.

"Where water is lacking," Vijayo said, "blossoms are also."

Balakrama said, "The people have brought what they have, yet even at this distance it seems the petals are small and poor in color."

As the sun rose, it still fell with splendor on the brazen roof of the storied monastery standing near the center of the city. Nearby, people went about their work; the streets and shops were filled with the sound of busy voices; but hardly any laughter was heard, as if the hearts of men and women were as low as the waters in the tanks.

The royal palace had many buildings. First the three brothers went to their own apartments. After bathing and dressing again as princes, they hurried to the handsome structure where the king lived. Here, before entering, they removed their sandals and set them in a careful row outside the doorway.

When at last they were admitted to their father, they had time for but a quick glance at him before they bowed their faces to the floor with deep respect. Yet in that instant the brothers saw Jaiya resting on a great couch and looking much older than they remembered him. His hair was white now, and many were the lines of care in his kindly face.

Permitted at once to rise, they stood in front of the king while Balakrama, for his brothers and himself, spoke first.

"Every day we have longed to see your noble face," he said. "So now our hearts overflow with gratitude that Your Majesty has called us home. Yet we grieve to find you, Sir, so ill. Moreover, in shame and sorrow we stand here, because we have failed most miserably in our search for the formula called *Death to Dragons*. Except for a tiny fragment with only the six lines already known to us, the words on the precious scroll were utterly destroyed by fire before we came upon them."

King Jaiya opened his eyes wide. Over his face passed an expression of deep disappointment, which he seemed, out of politeness, to be trying vainly to conceal.

Balakrama bowed and continued.

"Alas! Sir, we cannot show Your Majesty even the silver case of Aphoenicius. It was seized by the golden bird who flew away after filling it with naught but our own tears, wept over the wretched plight of the people of Kuhabad. So," he continued, "we can only beg your royal forgiveness as we return in robes of failure."

King Jaiya said, "Whatever has happened, I bid you welcome. My love for you was too strong to bear your absence any longer."

Then he questioned them concerning all their adventures of which he had not yet heard. So they told him at length about their encounter with the dragon king, the unexpected aid brought by the great bird, and concerning other happenings, too.

After some time had passed in this way, a royal servant appeared with a message. Slowly King Jaiya unfastened the letter, then evidently astonished, sat up straight. He looked at his three sons.

"Sped by swift couriers," he said, "here is good news from one of my officials. He says that on our shores lie multitudes of lifeless dragons, including a creature with a jewelled crown, but in the seas there are none."

The three princes stood silent with amazement as their father continued.

"This message also tells me that some of our people looking up into the sky have seen a great bird carrying a cylinder of silver. From it, as they watched, drops of some mysterious fluid fell into our tanks and canals."

The king's voice rose with excitement.

"Listen to this," he said, now reading from the scroll. "*'Wherever these drops have fallen, the waters seem to have risen like magic fountains. The people who have, are sharing with those who have not. Already Your Majesty's subjects, with raised spirits, are busy repairing the reservoirs and waterways.'*"

"What can this mean?" said the three princes almost at once.

"It means," King Jaiya said, "that my sons need not be ashamed to stand before their father. Although you have not brought me a written scroll with the formula, *Death to Dragons,* your tears of compassion for the poor and afflicted are the very potion itself. With help from the golden bird, they have not only spelled death for the fierce dragons but also seem to have brought us an abundance of life-giving water and new heart."

At these words the princes were filled with happiness. And their father found more than happiness, for his health returned quickly. And he rejoiced with all his people when soon a great rain fell upon the land, and the wide tanks, now well-repaired, were filled to overflowing.

In the days that followed, King Jaiya, after talking earnestly with the princes, gave his consent for the marriage of Vijayo to the accomplished and charming Princess Purandocht of Persia. In that country the emperor made him a royal governor in charge of one of the chief districts of his empire, and he sat on a silver throne.

Also, Prince Rajahsingha was given his father's permission to marry the beauteous Queen Parvathi. For years to come and in great felicity, he ruled by her side.

King Jaiya meanwhile received letters from many monarchs, each wishing to arrange a marriage for one of his daughters to His Royal Highness Prince Balakrama. But the love of this young man for fair Podihamine remained steadfast. In the simple garb of a mahout and riding upon Kandula with all of his fancy trappings laid aside, the oldest prince stopped to see her many times. Thus he learned that she, without knowing he was a prince, returned his affection.

Hearing of this, King Jaiya called the young woman to the palace, where full of surprise and wonder, she came with her father. When the king, who received her in kindly fashion, discovered that she was not only beautiful but was, like his oldest son, gentle with plants and living things, he spoke to Balakrama.

"Some day," he said, "you will rule in my place, and even now you bring me strength and comfort. With joy for your happiness, therefore, I consent to your marrying the fair Podihamine. She has her father's blessing and loves you well."

The wedding of Balakrama took place in Serendip with great rejoicing. The people marched through Anuradhapura in a glad parade. Adorned with jewelled trappings, at the head of it, walked Kandula. Later, rich and poor alike all feasted; and since there were no longer any dragons in the sea, storytellers came from many lands to entertain.

Thus, the three princes of Serendip all became rulers, each so filled with virtue, wisdom, and science that, governing well, he was much beloved.

As for the golden bird, some say that he was last seen flying high above the wild mountain valleys near the ancient and holy Peak of Great Serenity, and that as he flew, a thousand tears, falling from the cylinder of silver, turned into rubies, sapphires and emeralds. Others say that sometimes still, when least expected, the golden bird dips into sight, but is seen only by those who are looking up.

PANTOUM FOR THE GOLDEN BIRD

He flies, a jewel of surprise,
With sudden winging out of night.
For those who dream with lifted eyes
The golden bird may dip in sight.

With sudden winging out of night
As a thousand tears turn into gems,
The golden bird may dip in sight
To crown the brave with diadems.

As a thousand tears turn into gems
For those who dream with lifted eyes,
To crown the brave with diadems
He flies, a jewel of surprise.

Notes

"Serendip" is another name for the beautiful island of Ceylon, and from Serendip came the word *serendipity.* One of the happiest words in our language, it was coined by the English author, Horace Walpole, who lived from 1717 to 1797.

The Merriam-Webster unabridged dictionary defines it as *"The gift of finding valuable or agreeable things not sought for,"* and Walpole explained it in a letter of January 28, 1754. Alluding to a "fairy tale, called 'The Three Princes of Serendip,' " he wrote, "as their highnesses travelled, they were always making discoveries, by accidents and sagacity, of things which they were not in quest of . . ."

There are several versions of the tale. The one which he read was in French, published in Amsterdam in 1721 and entitled "Voyage . . . des trois princes de Serendip." A still earlier version was published in Italian in 1557.

The book you are reading contains new poems and a story which draws from a version of the tale in English called "The Travels and Adventures of Three Princes of Serendip . . . London, Printed for Will. Chetwood . . ." in 1722. It is also derived from other sources, including history, geography, mythology, and the happy idea of serendipity itself.

Although a fairy tale, the period of this story is in the fifth century A.D. in the royal days of Anuradhapura in Ceylon, the Sassanid Empire in Persia, and famous dynasties such as those of the Gupta Empire and the Vakatakas in the land of India.

If you would like to read more about Ceylon, Persia (Iran) and India, here is a list of some books you might enjoy:

Fairservis, Walter A., Jr. *India*. The World Publishing Company, 1961.

Modak, Manorama R. *The Land and the People of India*. J. B. Lippincott Company, rev. ed. 1952.

Spencer, Cornelia. *Made in India, the Story of India's People*. Alfred Knopf, 1953.

Taylor, Alice. *Iran*. Holiday House, 1955.

Weston, Christine. *Ceylon*. Charles Scribner's Sons, 1960.

Wilber, Donald N. *The Land and People of Ceylon*. J. B. Lippincott Company, 1963.

Acknowledgments

The author thanks all who cooperated with her in the undertaking of this book, including personnel in the Massachusetts public libraries of Arlington, Boston, Brookline and Medford, in the Cleveland Public Library and the Library of Congress, and in the following academic libraries: the Chinese-Japanese Library of the Harvard-Yenching Institute at Harvard University, the Baker, Houghton, Center for Middle East Studies, and Widener libraries of Harvard University, and the libraries of the Episcopal Theological School, Cambridge, Massachusetts and of Colby Junior College, New London, New Hampshire, and also in the Boston Athenaeum.

She also thanks the many individuals who helped with special information and in other ways, including Dr. Chandra Raj Amarasingham, Miss Chandra Bhatia, Dr. Carl Binger, Mrs. Paul J. Boylan, Miss Maheswari Candiah, Mrs. John B. Das, Mrs. Joseph F. Fletcher, Mrs. Edward V. Gulick, Mr. S. J. Gunasegaram, Mrs. William L. Hodges, Mr. Siri Jayaratne, Mrs. Ronald S. Johnson, Mr. Donald Junkins, Commander Richard D. King, Mrs. J. Laing, Mr. Wilmarth S. Lewis, Mrs. Loy L. Long, Mr. David McCord,

Miss Catherine E. McCormick, Mr. Laurence R. Moses, Mr. M. J. Perera, Mr. Theodore G. Remer, Miss Goolie Sadrieh, Miss Caroline Sauer, Mr. Nimalasiri Silva, Miss Elizabeth C. Smith, Mr. Jack M. Stein, Miss Judith E. Stromdahl, Miss Bharti Trivedi, Mr. Joseph M. Upton, Mrs. Samuel Zahl, and, very especially, her teachers of writing.

Elizabeth Jamison Hodges

was born in Atlanta, Georgia, and has lived in many cities of eastern and middle-western United States, in Puerto Rico, and in Japan, Manchuria, and China. She has also traveled extensively in Europe. After attending Radcliffe College and Simmons College of Library Science, she became a librarian and is now at Robbins Library in Arlington, Massachusetts.

Miss Hodges is interested in people, poetry, painting, politics, and international peace, all of which have contributed to this, her first book for children.